Praise for *A Study in Black Brew*:

"Who doesn't love a good Sherlock Holmes retelling? Now make it diverse, with wonderful lovable characters, an alien world, a dash of humour, and a lot of cosy vibes. And did I mention the space elves? Definitely not just for fans of the infamous detective duo, but everyone who enjoys cosy sci-fi and mysteries."

— Iris Retzlaff, author of *Moon's Lament*

"*A Study in Black Brew* is a Sherlockian mystery with a fresh sci-fi slant that enlivens a classic while paying homage to spirit of the original. A must read for fans of Conan Doyle who yearn for a modern twist."

— Kara Jorgenson, author of *The Reanimator's Heart*

"*A Study in Black Brew* is a story that lingers. It's full of Marie's signature wit and banter, presenting a layered plot that's pushed forward by a charming cast of characters."

— Nathaniel Luscombe, author of *Moon Soul*

"An alien Sherlock Holmes lets Howalt explore new aspects of the well-known characters. The relationship between the retired chemist Kellieth, who has a respiratory dysfunction, and the brilliant but also somewhat annoying and insensitive detective Raithan unfolds convincingly. Through Kellieth's narration we experience the struggle of living with a disability that is physically straining as well as a social problem because the wendek communicate their emotions through scent. Like Howalt's *Colibri Investigations* books it's a soft SF cozy murder mystery with a lot of seriousness to it. A nice cup of black brew, well rounded but still sharp."

— Jane Mondrup, author of *Zeitgeist* and *Zoi*

"Writing a great retelling is the art of presenting the expected, and often sentimental, in a fresh and exciting way. In *A Study in Black Brew*, Marie does this with flair and heart. While the story is recognizably based on Sir Arthur Conan Doyle's *A Study in Scarlet*, everything is shifted to unveil an alien world of excitement and danger, while making ample room for cozier moments and lovable characters. There is nothing elementary about this charming detective story. Well done Marie!"

—J. Cornelius, author of *Remembering Demons and Catching Spiders*

"A futuristic take on a classic detective that's as fresh as the brew. And if you're someone with an invisible disability, be prepared to be visible like never before. And I never had the same fangirl attraction to Sherlock and Watson in popular remakes. But reading this? I get it."

— Aden Ng, author of *The Chronicles of Tearha*

"Marie Howalt does queer and neurodivergent justice to Sherlock Holmes' legacy in the latest novel, *A Study in Black Brew.* Highly entertaining, clever, with a true dose of mystery and deep empathy, *A Study in Black Brew* will satisfy any reader who enjoys puzzle mysteries and a modern reflection on the true personal cost of handicap and neurodiversity. Totally recommended."

— Seb Doubinsky, author of *The Sum Of All Things*

"Who says you can't touch the classics? Marie Howalt's queer sci-fi remix of one of Sherlock Holmes' best-known adventures is a brilliant new spin on Conan Doyle's Great Detective and his faithful assistant, full of effortless word-building and irresistible characters. Pour yourself a cup of black brew and cozy up with it."

— Brandon Getz, author of *Lars Breaxface: Werewolf in Space*

"*A Study in Black Brew* is a vibrant Sherlock Holmes retelling with some great characters in an interesting world. I enjoyed the chemistry between the alien cast and trying to remember or guess where the story was going."

— K. P. Kilbride, author of *Spaceships Passing in the Night*

Also by Marie Howalt

Colibri Investigations

The Wenamak Web (2024)
Assassins & Olympians (2023)
The Stellar Snow Job (2022)

Moonless

Training Wheels (2021)
Heart of the Storm (2021)
Seeking Shelter (2020)
We Lost the Sky (2019)

A STUDY IN BLACK BREW

MARIE HOWALT

Denver, Colorado

Published in the United States by:
Spaceboy Books LLC
1627 Vine Street
Denver, CO 80206
www.readspaceboy.com

Cover art designed by Miblart

ISBN: 978-1-951393-48-9
First printed May 2025

A Study in Black Brew is a light read and suitable for most readers. It does, however, include references to intoxication, abduction, obstructed breathing, guns, minor character death, blood, violence, ableism and speciesist language.

For everyone who lives with a chronic illness or disability.
This one is for you.

Chapter I
RETURN TO NANTHEAM

They say life is a string of chances held together with grit and guided by passion, and who am I to disagree? Certainly, grit and passion were among the main ingredients in my decision to enroll at the Institute of Science on our species' home planet, Ganmak. I had only just completed my doyen degree in chemistry when the Wendek Planetary Development Agency advertised a position as a field chemist on Almaimak, which is our most recent settlement. The job description seemed to fit a person of my qualifications, and though many may consider it a prestigious and perhaps overly ambitious job for such a young scientist as myself, I was determined to carve out a career in my field. It meant leaving Ganmak for at least two years, but I was without serious attachments, and this was the path I had been pursuing ever since the accident I suffered during my required school years. Some experiences leave you with an inevitable choice between avoidance and obsession. Clearly, I chose obsession.

Sadly, grit and passion will only get you so far, and my dreams of honor and promotion in that field were shattered before long.

The initial reports from Almaimak had cleared the planet for settlement, but my team was among the first to live there, and we were only starting to learn what dangers lurked on the new world. To begin with, I expected the atmospheric composition, slightly higher in oxygen than on Ganmak, to be beneficial for my condition, but while that was true in theory, the irregularities of the weather proved hazardous to say the least.

I had only been on Almaimak for a few months when my research team and I were stuck outside during a particularly violent dust storm that lasted for days. We always brought standard safety equipment on excursions, but the filters on our facemasks were simply not up to the task of protecting us against the hostile environment. It was troublesome to the others on my team, but life-threatening to me. I am not exaggerating when I say I might well have lost my life if not for my colleagues' skills and care.

While recovering from this ordeal, I was struck down by the so-called Almaimak plague, which is a virus that is not normally considered serious. But for someone with a compromised respiratory system, it too proved nearly fatal. As a result, I was so weak and emaciated that a medical board determined that, as soon as I was well enough, not a day should be lost in sending me back to Ganmak.

So there I was, despondent and without a direction for the first time in my life. I had no family and only few friends on Ganmak and was therefore free as air, as the saying awkwardly goes because for obvious reasons, it rubs me entirely the wrong way. In any case, I decided to go back to the planet's capital city Nantheam in the hope that once I was well enough to take a job again, I would be able to find a position that fit my skills there. I knew it would never be as exciting as exploring a strange new world, but I could settle for perhaps a teaching job or a mundane research job.

When I arrived, I rented a fully furnished apartment in the Deith District, a fashionable area conveniently in the center of the great city. I did not consider the financial aspects because, quite frankly, I was still too marred by my recent illness to care. It quickly turned out, however, that I would have to reconsider because the benefits provided by the health services were not great. This was partly due to a dispute over who should support me since I was originally part of the Menal minority on Tewamak, had lived for years as a citizen on Ganmak, and had fallen ill on Almaimak. I was hoping to have a job and be able to support myself financially before the lengthy legal process was over.

In any case, I was beginning to look for cheaper lodgings, but had no luck until by coincidence, I met a former acquaintance from the Institute of Science.

I was waiting for a cup of black brew at the human-style eatery close to my temporary home where I liked to spend my idle afternoons and, if I am honest, too many of my funds. It was called Diogenes and was staffed by both wendek and humans. Allegedly, the name referred to a cynical human philosopher who lived in a barrel. I assume he is a fictional character.

In any case, Teimforth SeinnunWanneinth had never been a friend of mine, but the mere sight of a familiar face was a relief. It somehow made me feel more at home in the city I thought I had left behind, even if it was only one person who had occasionally asked for my advice when exams were approaching since I was a little older and further advanced in my studies. Luckily, Teimforth appeared happy to see me as well.

She had changed her hair from the turquoise she sported during our student days to a darker green close to my own, and we had styled our hair similarly as well, the front part gathered in a practical knot at the back of our heads and a loose braid spilling down our backs. As we laughed at this coincidence, I entertained the notion that perhaps she was as lonely as I, though this should prove to be simple projection.

"I hope you don't mind me asking," Teimforth said as she joined me at the table with a cup of steaming tea, a human drink that was considered more palatable by people in general than my own choice of beverage, "but are you all right?"

I could have said yes, and I certainly was more all right than I had been in the recent past, but I saw no point in denying the apparent.

My skin has always been a pale grey compared to the majority of Nantheam's inhabitants, but it had an unhealthy tint to it now, and I was undeniably more gaunt and probably smelled more exhausted than she remembered from our late-night study sessions.

So I summarized my time on Almaimak in the way that anyone who has suffered a blow to their physical or mental health will be familiar with. We tend to downplay our wounds and hide them behind amusing anecdotes as not to make the listener too uncomfortable.

Yet, Teimforth understood the depth of my troubles and appeared genuinely sorry for me. It wasn't something I generally encouraged if I could help it. When you have lived with a chronic illness for as long as I have, you just want to get on with life without dwelling on it more than necessary because it is always there like a demanding passenger riding your shoulders, taking up space whether you want it to or not.

"Oh, Creators. I'm sorry, Kellieth. That's a lot," she said after a long pause. "So you came back to Ganmak. What are your plans now?"

I smiled, glad to be moving on from my troubles. "Well, I need to look for a more affordable place to live while I get sorted out."

"What a coincidence," she said. "I'm looking for a new place too! Everything is so expensive in Nantheam these days. But hold on, I found something in the Monarth Park District earlier..." She swiped at her personal adaptive touch communication hub, or patch as the device is colloquially called, on her wrist and began to search. She was wearing a brand new model that looked a lot more decorative than mine, but I am more willing to prioritize functionality over fashion than most people you expect to find sipping foreign beverages in the fancy parts of Nantheam.

As I considered her words, the scene suddenly felt like the beginning of a romantic comedy where two old school mates unexpectedly reunite, move in together and eventually hook up. And as happy as seeing a familiar face had made me a moment ago, I felt reluctant at the idea of living with Teimforth. I wanted a fresh start, and I was pretty sure watching another chemist having a great career while I had nothing would not be beneficial for me.

"Ah, there we are!" she said and pulled up a semitransparent display from her patch to float in midair between us.

The building in the picture was old. I'm not an architect or a historian, but it appeared to be from that period when chunky meant wealthy and everything had to have rounded corners, and getting off the ground to get away from the smells of old-fashioned groundwheeler exhaust fumes was a consideration. There was a staircase leading from the street to the front door. If any modernizations had taken place, they were invisible to my untrained eye.

I cleared my throat. "I think I rather need to live alone for a while," I began.

Teimforth stared at me and breathed in. "What? Oh, you thought..." She laughed. "I'm sorry, but no. My wife and I want another child, and we both feel we need a bigger place before the baby is born. This house has been split into two apartments with a traditional common area on each floor, and two adjacent ones were free when I saw the ad, so I figured we could get both. But when I contacted the administrator, it turned out someone else was already interested in one of them. And besides, it's a rental. We're looking to buy. I thought it might be more suitable for you."

Well, now I was embarrassed. I hadn't even thought of asking about her personal life. "Oh, congratulations," I managed without specifying whether I was congratulating her on having a wife, a child and preparing for one more, or the funds to buy a house. Probably all of it. "And thank you." I looked more closely at the house. "Would you mind sending the ad over?"

"Of course not," Teimforth said. She opened a connection to my patch and forwarded it.

The apartments came with basic furnishings which was the standard for rentals in Nantheam. And the place was fairly affordable. If I cut some of my expenses, like going to Diogenes for black brew instead of getting some cheap instant powder and making my own, it was doable on my budget even now.

"I talked to the guy who wanted to rent the other apartment to see if he was committed, though," Teimforth said.

"Though?" I asked.

"Yes, well, he is a bit..." She wrinkled her nose.

"Smelly?" I suggested.

"I don't know. We only talked on our patches," she said. "But there was something off about him. I don't know. Just... Don't blame me if he turns out to be a weirdo."

"All right," I said. 'Something off' could be anything, really. And I was fairly certain I could not afford to turn down a good offer on the grounds that a former co-student of mine found my neighbor a little odd.

Later that day, I contacted the administrator of the building, a woman called Hussa. That was a Lai name, and I always have to remind myself that their naming conventions aren't like the traditional Menal or Synal ones. Our primary name consists of a personal component followed by our family name, and our secondary name is based on our date of birth. Hussa was her family name rather than her personal name. Interestingly, several of our fellow sentient species, like humans and draevere, favor a similar naming pattern to that of Lai. But I digress.

Hussa was of middle age or a little older. Her hair was undyed, but a beautiful, glossy silver tone. Her eyes were a light, almost greenish yellow that crinkled when she smiled at me.

I introduced myself and explained my reason for contacting her.

"You do realize that this is not really..." She trailed off, then began again, "You are most welcome to have a look at the apartment, Doyen, but I don't want to waste your time. It is an old house, charming but lacking some of the conveniences of more modern buildings."

I breathed out in annoyance. Had she somehow noticed my disability and thought I could not even make it up a short flight of stairs without getting winded? But no, of course not. She had addressed me as Doyen, and an academic of that title ought to have a well-paid position that would buy them a far more luxurious home. "I saw the stills of it," I said quickly. "I think it looks like a lovely place."

"It is," Hussa agreed. "I live on the upper floor myself. Every apartment has its own toilet and washroom, a bedroom, a kitchen, a living room and, of course, access to a common room. There is a wonderful bakery a short walk down the street that does traditional Menal pastries as well as more experimental ones. If you need a place to meditate or get some pure air, you can easily walk to Monarth Park. And the Verdant is only a short groundwheeler ride away."

I smiled. I had looked at a map, and it was true that both the park and the nature reservation were close, but my personal preoccupation had been with how far it was from the river that cut through Nantheam because the area near the Ometha was often humid and foggy, and I would prefer to avoid that. Luckily, it was was several kilometers. "It sounds like the perfect place for me. I am currently between jobs due to recent health complications," I added because if she lived in the same building, she might wonder why I did not appear to work, and I would rather not have to answer questions later on.

"Oh, I am sorry to hear that. Perhaps a quiet neighborhood is exactly what you need, then," she said.

"Yes, I think so," I agreed. Especially if you substituted 'cheap' for 'quiet'.

Chapter II
RAITHAN WEINZALNEINTH

Only a handful of days after my first conversation with Hussa, I was standing in the street outside my new home with all that was left of my old life stuffed into a modest heap of bags and boxes.

Groundwheelers passed behind me at intervals, their occupants going about their own business and only using this particular street as a means to get from one location to the next. All in all, it was a fairly quiet street with no public transport routes and only few pedestrians.

I took a deep breath, or as deep a breath as my current condition would allow. It was time to get started. I picked up a box full of my most treasured belongings and started up the stairs to the front door. My retina scan for the lock had not gone through yet, so I had been issued with a temporary key card. I balanced the box carefully while trying to get a grip on the card in my pocket. It had, of course, lodged itself beneath my inhaler, but I managed to get it up and fumble the door open.

Another, albeit short, flight of stairs led to a landing with two identical doors. They were made from wood, an interesting extravagance typical of their time, and were operated manually. The one on the right led to my apartment, and my new neighbor lived behind the left. In the back of the house where the common room was located, the two were conjoined. I had hoped to meet my neighbor when I inspected the building a few days prior, but he had not been around then.

I used another temporary key card to get into my apartment and placed my box on the battered piece of furniture right inside. It tried to be a table, a bench and a chest of drawers at the same time. Functional, but not a pretty thing. Next to it was a sweetly fragrant fern that had also seen better days. I moved the plant to prop the door open. The contents of the pocket in my jacket dug awkwardly into my side, so I tossed my inhaler onto the box and left to get the next load. One might argue that I should have hired someone to help me move, but I was trying to cut down on expenses, and I could not bring myself to request assistance from the local community center. I was not that bad off. Or so I thought.

"Do you need a hand?" asked a voice behind me as I was summoning the strength for my third trip up the stairs. Startled, I looked around.

The speaker was a good head taller than I and extremely handsome. He had long, blue hair that suited the warm hue of his dark grey skin very well indeed and eyes nearly the shade of a deep scarlet fathe. Sartorially, his choices were so bold and beautiful that I felt strangely underdressed in my casual moving-day-appropriate almost threadbare brown and blue attire. The man's dark red jacket was cinched at the waist with a lovely sash and open to reveal a black shirt with red accents and a neckwrap tied in a formal knot at the side. His trousers matched the shirt, which made me think he must be on his way to or from a formal occasion. However, that assumption contrasted with a bag flung over his shoulder and a large box that must be at least as heavy as my burden.

"Thank you," I said, trying not to wheeze, "but I'm all right."

The man sized me up. I saw him breathe in everything about me, my discomfort and fatigue laid bare to his senses along with my gender identity and a hint of the black brew I consumed earlier that day. His feelings were opaque to my nose, of course. At least it saves me from a lot of awkwardness that I am nearly always able to detect the gender markers in other people's perfumes. "All right," he said lightly and turned to leave.

"Do you live here?" I called after him.

"Yes," he replied, looking back over his shoulder briefly. And then he continued up the stairs at an enviable speed.

Was this my new neighbor, then? Belatedly, I thought I ought to have introduced myself. I followed him at a slower pace, half wishing I had taken him up on the offer anyway. It had merely seemed so inconvenient for him to have to put down his own things or go up with them and then return to me.

When I emerged once more, it had begun to rain. Admittedly, the word does not convey the nature of late summer in Nantheam. One moment, it is a fresh and windy day, and the next, a torrent of water is pouring out of the skies. These downpours usually only last a few hours at the most, but a few hours was more than enough to ruin those of my belongings that were still outside, and I knew from experience that the drop in air pressure was less than beneficial for my constitution.

I ran down the stairs, picked up another box and made my way up, taking some of the steps two at a time, slipping and almost falling twice. I was breathing hard. As fit as I had kept before going to Almaimak, I was frightfully frail now.

The only items I had left were a single box and a traveling bag with wheels that were useless on stairs, so I hurried out once more. The rain rendered the city murky, but I was uncomfortably aware that it was growing darker and dimmer than it logically ought to. I stopped for a moment, trying to force air into my lungs, but my throat felt constricted. I held my breath to gain control, but it did nothing to help. My heart was pounding as if breaking its cage would help me get enough oxygen. This wasn't going to go away on its own.

I reached for my inhaler and then wanted to kick myself. You would think that even a humble scientist such as myself would have the foresight to keep it on their body when pushing themself physically. Apparently I was a dimdek.

I turned, the world spun, and I missed both the handle of the old-fashioned door and my step entirely.

The next thing I knew was someone talking to me through the haze in my mind. "Come on. Breathe out slowly."

I made a feeble attempt.

"There you go," the voice said, and my inhaler somehow materialized in front of me. I am not sure I had the capacity to even operate that simple mechanism at that moment, but the person with me was holding it and pressed the button to release my emergency medication. "Hold your breath for a moment. And breathe out again as slowly as you can."

Under normal circumstances, I would have scoffed at someone guiding me through a procedure I both knew the theory behind and had done so many times before, but right then, I absolutely needed the guidance. I latched onto that calm and soft voice and followed its directions, only managing not to faint again because of it.

I coughed, but the voice was persistent and stayed collected. And after a little while, my breathing slowed and came more easily. The fog was starting to dissipate too. I was sprawled on my back, soaked with rain and sweat, and the handsome man I met earlier was next to me on the stairs, holding my inhaler and supporting my head. "You —" I gasped and then had to take another deep breath.

"You were only out for a minute," the man said. "I hate to rush you, but I suspect the cold rain and humidity out here are not too healthy for you. Can you stand?"

"My things," I said instead of thanking him. I think I hadn't quite wrapped my mind around what was happening.

The man indicated understanding, grabbed my hand, placed the inhaler in it and then got to his feet. I watched him dash down the stairs, pick up my remaining belongings as if they weighed nothing and vault back up. He opened the door, placed my stuff on the floor inside and then proceeded to help me to my feet.

I hated how feeble I felt. He was probably my neighbor, and this was his first impression of me. A scrawny youth fumbling about with their belongings and fainting in the pouring rain, desperately needing assistance. So much for wanting my condition not to be a defining feature in the eyes of others.

The man helped me up the stairs and to the open door of my apartment.

"I'm fine now. Thank you," I said, disentangling myself from his support, although, or maybe because, I was trembling.

"I would loathe to leave you on your own just yet," he replied and followed me into the apartment.

I went through the entrance area to the room that would become my living room once I got settled in. I sat down in a chair that I wanted to replace as soon as possible. "I really am fine," I told him reedily. It was not entirely true. An episode like that always leaves me fatigued and shaky, in addition to which I was also shocked by my own negligence. It could have killed me. "You might have saved my life," I added, embarrassing as it was to admit. "I'm Kellieth ReinAraneinth, by the way. I suspect I'm your new neighbor."

The man smiled and bowed gracefully over his upturned hands in the traditional greeting. His being soaked with rainwater that dripped from the tip of his nose did nothing to subtract from his poise. "Well deducted," he said, sounding like he wanted to laugh. I wished my sense of smell was up to par so I could decide if he was making fun of me. "My name is Raithan WeinZalneinth."

If you were inclined to attach meaning to birthdates, Raithan's last name indicated a day auspicious to change. But then, my own was one of honor, and here I was, drenched to the skin, slightly dazed and quite embarrassed.

"You should drink something. The twa is almost ready," Raithan continued.

"The... twa?" I asked.

"Stay there and keep breathing," he told me. He turned and went into the tiny kitchen where I could hear him bustle about. When he returned, it was with two chipped and steaming cups, one of which he placed in my hands.

My mind was replaying the timeline of what had happened. "I have to ask," I said as I accepted one of the cups, "how did you get my inhaler that quickly? How did you even know I had one? And... where did you get the twa?"

Raithan's face lit up in a genuine smile. "Simple enough. When we first met, I noticed the discoloration of your fingernails indicating a lack of oxygen. You were exhibiting other clear symptoms of a respiratory defect too, but as you were disinclined to accept my help then, I estimated I would have time to take my own things up and make preparations before you were in any danger." He raised his cup to his lips and blew on the surface of the twa. "The door to your apartment was open, and I spotted your inhaler readily enough when I peered in."

"And the twa?" I asked, even as I was trying to process all this.

"Well, I thought I still had a little time before you came to any harm, so I put your kettle on. There was a jar of twa on your kitchen counter, which I suspect the previous tenant must have left. It smells fresh enough. But you can't easily tell that, can you?"

I blinked. "How do you know that?" Asthma and similar respiratory conditions were not normally indicative of anosmia or hyposmia.

"You did not smell the twa when I handed you the cup. I have never known anyone with a properly working sense of smell not to do that."

"Right..." I muttered. Now he probably thought I was a vapor addict. Too many hard drugs and your sense of smell as well as your breathing would suffer. Brilliant.

"I expect a lab accident led to your condition?" Raithan asked.

"I— Yes," I admitted. "But how..?" I was sounding like a looped clip at this point.

Raithan only smiled. "Drink your twa. You need fluids and

warmth."

I did as he asked with the unnerving feeling that he was the sort of person who could somehow make people do what he wanted without the effort of threats or any kind of authority over them because of his good looks and earnest voice. But the twa did help. In general, twa has many positive effects due to its chemical composition. It is a natural stimulant because of the aneiphere, which is not unlike caffeine, but a lot more healthy for the wendek constitution. Personally, I am partial to black brew because it has similar effects and a less delicate quality which means I don't feel I am missing out every time I have it like I do with twa.

"You are a chemist, right?" my neighbor asked.

"I— Yes. But how..?" I said. Again.

"Brilliant," Raithan said under his breath. "I've always felt I was lacking in that field myself."

"What?" I asked.

Raithan drained his own cup of twa and put it on the table. "I will take my leave now. You seem to have recovered enough to be on your own, but do be careful in the future. Thank you for the twa, Kellieth." And then he was, indeed, leaving.

"I— Thank you for saving my life," I said to the empty room. I don't expect he heard me.

Chapter III
THE SCIENCE OF DEDUCTION

The following day, I found myself outside my neighbor's door with a cake from the local bakery Hussa had recommended. There was a total of five possible reasons for this. One: I wanted to show my appreciation for Raithan's help the previous day. Two: I hated feeling indebted to anyone, and this would get the debt cleared somewhat. Three: Raithan never answered my questions properly and I wanted answers. Four: I found the man extremely attractive. Five: I was lonely in Nantheam and hoped to make a friend. In the interest of honesty, it was probably a mix of them all.

Raithan opened the door. He was wearing remarkably little. A pair of loose pants and nothing else. It was no wonder he had been running up and down the stairs with little effort with that physique. "There you are," he said as if this was a prearranged meeting.

"Um, yes. I was... That is to say..." I faltered. Possibly, I should have rehearsed this.

"Come on in, then," he said, holding the ancient door open. "You will forgive my casual appearance. When I realized you were going to be here so early, I opted for making a batch of twa instead of dressing for the occasion."

"I... what?" I asked. It was, in fact, not very early at all. I had breakfasted quite a while before I went to the bakery. "You were expecting me?" I said.

"Oh yes. Shall I take that?"

"Please," I said and held out the box. "It's a cake," I added, horrendously unnecessarily, "to thank you for your help yesterday."

Raithan smiled. "I see," he said, and regardless of his earnest expression, I did not need to be able to pick up on discreet pheromones to discern he was amused on my account. "Please make yourself comfortable."

He left in the direction of the kitchen, taking the cake with him. Assuming he didn't intend for me to make myself comfortable in the narrow entrance area, I took off my shoes and made my way to the living room. Raithan's apartment was, in terms of layout, a mirror image of mine. But that was where the similarities ended. The furniture was functional enough but a little on the austere side. Clean, straight lines and a color scheme that was mostly white and dark brown with a few primary colors thrown into the mix. The interior of Raithan's apartment was, in other words, in stark contrast to the building's old-fashioned exterior. The art on the walls was modern too, and to my eye, it seemed that it had been selected more for fitting the style of the room than artistic or sentimental value. In any case, this apartment looked a great deal more aesthetically coherent than mine at the present. It did not, however, give me any clues about my neighbor except possibly his favorite colors. I'm not sure what I had expected. Stills of his friends and family? There was none in sight.

My searching gaze fell upon one incongruous item. It was a case resting against the wall in one corner. It looked old and battered and had the vague shape of a musical instrument, possibly a mewienn. Was my neighbor a musician?

"Here we go," Raithan said as he returned, balancing the quai berry cake on a large plate on one elegant hand and somehow carrying two smaller plates and two cups in the other. He was also wearing a shirt now, even if the flimsy material and the fact that it was unbuttoned to his sternum did little to change the general appearance of what he called casual attire.

"Oh, I wasn't inviting myself over for cake!" I protested, realizing the meaning of the two plates and two cups.

My host put the cake down on the table in the center of the room. "Yes, you were," he said. "I don't mind. I don't have any plans for today."

"You don't have a job you need to do to, or..?" I probed, clumsily.

"No," Raithan said. "You look a lot better today, Kellieth, but do sit down, anyway." He left the room again to, presumably, get the aforementioned twa and a knife for the cake.

I sat and tried not to fidget. The seat of the couch was soft and pleasant, centuries of ergonomic engineering hidden under the plain fabric.

Raithan returned once more. This time, he sat down in the chair on the opposite side of the table. I watched his hands as he poured twa for us both and sliced the cake with surgical precision using a knife that looked sharper than any normal kitchen utensil had any right to be. Two glazed berries adorning the cake were cut in half and spilled their juice down its pale pink sides. He put one slice in front of me and another in front of himself and then began to eat without further ado.

I raised the cup and breathed in.

"You don't have to do that," Raithan said.

"I *can* smell," I said. "Just not as well as other people. This is mynth twa, and it smells very good."

"Still, you only do that out of politeness. Your hyposmia means you don't get anything out of it." He raised his own cup, and I watched him with some envy as he clearly was able to derive a pleasurable sense of calm from the aroma.

"That reminds me," I said, a horrible at best and nonexistent segue at worst, "How did you know I'm a chemist?"

Raithan's smile was brilliant, as if he were pleased I remembered that little exchange. "A lucky guess?" he said.

"No," I replied. "Do you appreciate how many occupations exist? The chances of you randomly guessing mine are minimal."

"All right," he conceded, "it wasn't pure guesswork."

He popped a piece of cake into his mouth, closed his eyes and chewed slowly and deliberately. His lips curved into a smile, and he opened his eyes again. "Oh, Kellieth, you spoil me. This is delicious."

"I'm glad you like it. Hussa praised the local bakery, and I understand why." It was a very good cake indeed. I was part delighted and part worried for my future health that a bakery this great was right down the street from my new home. "So, my profession?"

"All right," Raithan said and licked a stray crumb off his thumb. "Your boxes had baggage labels from Almaimak. As that planet is only in the process of being settled now, chances were you are a researcher as you do not strike me as someone involved in heavy manual labor. Of course, you could be in administration or some other scientific field, but you have a few scars on your right hand that look like acid burns. And your respiratory dysfunction was, I assume, caused by a lab accident."

"I..." I began with absolutely no clue where the sentence was headed. "There could have so many other causes," I protested weakly. "I could have been born with this."

"Perhaps. Though if it was hereditary or even a random defect, it would probably have been screened and remedied before you were born. In any case, I was right."

I studied my host intently. He was absolutely correct about all of it. I almost asked him if he thought the lab accident was the direct cause of my being here and not on Almaimak now.

"No," Raithan said as if he were reading my mind too, "you are experiencing a flare up, which I expect is the reason for your leaving your post on Almaimak. But your problem is not in itself new."

"How did you..?" I spluttered.

"Simple deduction," Raithan told me in a way that can only be described as smug.

"You remind me of *Worra & Darith*," I muttered.

At this, Raithan's smile disappeared entirely. "Absolutely not."

"Perhaps not so much Darith," I amended, because admittedly, Worra was the brain of that popular fictional crime-solving duo. "But you seem to be as clever as Worra."

Raithan still did not look happy. "I'm not sure that's much of a compliment," he said. "Worra is purely fictional, and the way crimes are solved in that show is dumbed down and fed to the audience so everybody can follow. And then the plot is presented to make the recipients believe that they are extremely clever for being able to guess along and understand everything because the characters are supposed to be more intelligent than the average person."

That was a monologue I had not seen coming. I only meant to praise his skills, and his response to the compliment was uncivil. I all but slammed my cup onto the table. "Well, excuse me for being dumb enough to appreciate such vulgar entertainment," I said.

"Oh, my dear Doyen Kellieth ReinAraneinth," Raithan said, "You are hardly dumb."

I did not acknowledge the backhanded attempt at a compliment. "Right," I said instead, "it's just that you happen to be a clever investigator in the Nantheam peace corps yourself."

"No," Raithan replied a little too quickly.

"Actually," I went on, "You haven't told me what you do, and seeing as the only thing I can successfully deduce is a chemical formula, my nose is blocked here."

"Haven't I?" he mused. He knew perfectly well that was the case. He glanced down at his patch, and his brow furrowed briefly. "Oh, but you will have to excuse me cutting our chat short. I have a meeting I need to get ready for."

"I thought you didn't have any plans for today?" I asked as casually as possible.

"I didn't. But now I do," Raithan said. And I absolutely could not tell whether he really had received a notification by an employer, or if it was a ploy to keep me from asking more questions.

I am not the kind of person who enjoys idle vacations. I get bored when I don't have something to occupy my attention, and with how ragged my health still was, I could not even get the physical exercise my body needed to release a satisfying amount of endorphins.

It is a testament to how fed up I already was with not having any real research and experiments to do that Raithan WeinZalneinth became my object of study over the next half month. While I did understand the 'something off' that Teimforth had mentioned, he was an agreeable enough neighbor who never did anything to disturb me. The only potentially annoying noise he made was with the instrument in the case I had noticed upon my first visit, indeed a mewienn, and I was not bothered by it at all, except for the small aside that it made me miss dancing.

When we met in the hallway between our apartments or in that old-fashioned common room joining them, one of us would strike up conversation, and although I always walked away from these encounters feeling like Raithan had learned a great deal about me and I nothing about him, I still enjoyed them.

He did keep strange hours. Some days, he would leave the house before I was even awake and not be back until late in the night. Other days, I would not hear a sound from his apartment at all, and I found myself fretting ever so slightly that perhaps something was amiss with him. I did wonder if perhaps he was enjoying recreational vapors, but if he did so, my nose did not pick up on it.

As time went on, Raithan and I began to spend time together over a shared meal in the common room quite often. The furnishings were worn but of better quality than in my apartment and of a heavy style that fit the building well. I entertained the idea that everything in the room had been there since the first occupants moved in centuries ago, but I suspect the furniture would have been completely threadbare if that were the case.

Now, besides being bored, I honestly do enjoy cooking, so the food was mostly my doing. I like putting a spin of wendek spices on imported cuisines of other species, as well as making a hearty, traditional ripeth soup as refined as it can be. Yet, I am always a bit self-conscious about my culinary experiments as a scent compromised chemist.

Regardless, Raithan consistently complimented my food. Curious, and still trying to figure out what it was that he did for a living, I once suggested that perhaps he would like to do the cooking next time. At this, my neighbor laughed as if I'd made a joke. "Trust me when I say that's an experience you'd rather forgo!" he said.

This made me reflect on whether I actually did trust him, and also whether his lack of cooking skills might be the reason he so readily accepted and apparently delighted in my cooking.

"But you are right to ask," he added. "I have been accepting your kindness without any regards for your financial situation."

"That's not what I was trying to say," I protested, probably looking and smelling embarrassed. "We do live in a time when basic foodstuff is available at prices anyone can afford." And that was true. On Ganmak, imported goods, quality spices and fine cuisine can be pricey to say the least, but government regulations keep the costs of basic ingredients and ready-made meals very low. As it was, I spent more units on basic black brew powder than I would on twa of decent quality, but that was entirely my own choice and hardly something my neighbor influenced.

"Nevertheless," Raithan cut into my thoughts. "I can't let you feed me so often without repaying you."

I bit my lip because I would certainly not go to such awkward lengths as to tell him that his intriguing company was payment enough.

"Ah," Raithan said, smiling broadly. "I understand."

"What?" I asked.

My neighbor merely patted my shoulder. "I will make it up to you, my dear Kellieth."

The next day, an overflowing bag of groceries stood in front of my door in the hallway. There was a card stuck carelessly into it. And I was surprised to find that the text on it was handwritten in an antiquated calligraphy style that perhaps my great-great grandparents might have learned as a matter of course. The card said:

Dear Kellieth,

This is not payment for your efforts to keep me fed; it is merely a small contribution. Please allow me to pay you back by satisfying your curiosity, but grant me a little time to happen upon the opportune moment.

Faithfully,
Raithan

Chapter IV
THE SALEK GARDENS MYSTERY

"Are you busy?" Raithan asked when I opened the door of my apartment at his insistent knock.

It was a far earlier time of day than my neighbor habitually was up for, but he looked perfectly awake and dressed for an outing. Most of his hair was swept back in a mass of small braids gathered by a ribbon with only a few strands escaping to frame his face, and he was wearing a, for him, subtle dark purple suit with a black sash around his waist. I had slept poorly that night, haunted by dreams of being caught alone in a dust storm. I had woken up sweating and struggling to breathe and had needed to use my inhaler twice. As a result, I was feeling a tad uncharitable. "Don't you already know if I'm busy as well as... as my shoe size?" I said.

Raithan glanced down at my feet. "14?" he asked. "You own one pair of boots and two pairs of shoes, and you favor one of them. But... what does your footwear have to do with anything?"

Of course he was right about my shoe size and humble amount of footwear. "Yes, well, I thought you might like to dazzle me with your insight."

Raithan leaned against the door frame with a smile that should be banned from polite company. "Am I," he asked, "dazzling you?"

"Are you actually angling for compliments right now?" I asked, hoping I wasn't smelling as flustered as I felt.

"Anyway, are you coming?" he continued.

"You haven't even told me where you are going," I said.

"You wanted to know what I do. I'm going to show you."

How could I possibly resist that offer?

A few minutes later, we were going through the morning traffic in Raithan's groundwheeler. I hadn't known he owned one, and it surprised me that someone who rented a fairly cheap apartment could afford such a vehicle of their own. And not just any groundwheeler. It was a sleek, dark red one that sat low in the street and looked very expensive indeed. I am no motor aficionado, but I could tell it was a new model and of a quality brand.

The luxuriously soft seat was almost hugging me, and the safety restraints were snug against my body in a way that felt more comforting than restricting. I sat next to Raithan, looking out at Nantheam and trying to figure out where we were going as he drove. We left our own district soon enough and traversed one of the bridges that cross the Ometha. They have been built over a period of centuries; the newest is only about my age. Each bridge is a trademark of its respective construction period's distinctive architectural style, and the one Raithan chose matched the building we lived in in terms of heavy stonework. Nantheam grew up around the river, and even today is it used for transport of local goods. I watched a ship sailing toward the commercial harbor to the south until we reached the other side of the river and Raithan slowed down at a crossing. Through the front window of the groundwheeler, I watched pedestrians cross. Some were looking distractedly at their patches. One young person was carrying a pet transportation case, and I could just make out the snout and one wingtip of a syraxh inside. An elderly couple were holding hands and chatting animatedly. Our city is a diverse one, and this crossing was a slice of life that gave us a view of people of different skin tones, ages, sizes and builds. I spotted a single person wearing formal white. Another had their hair cropped short. There was a group of åayu tourists who looked slightly intimidated by the mass of much taller wendek around them.

"Oh, by the way," Raithan said as if the thought had only now occurred to him. "How are you with dead bodies?"

"Excuse me?" I ejaculated.

"Dead bodies. I assume the smell is not as bothersome to you as to someone with a keener nose, but what about the sight?"

"How... dead?" I managed.

"Quite dead."

"Yes, well, I meant *dead how*," I said. "Are we talking a really old person in a hospice who has lived a fulfilling life, or the victim of a gruesome murder?"

"It's not that gruesome," Raithan mused.

"But it is a murder victim?"

"I hope so," Raithan said.

"What?"

"I mean," he explained, "if it's not a crime, it's not my table, and then someone is wasting my time."

I opted for not replying. So Raithan WeinZalneinth was an investigator working in the fatality department? He had led me to believe he was not in the peace corps.

"Is there anything I should know about this... murder case?" I asked.

"Not really, but let me give you a quick summary. A few hours after midnight, a peace corps officer on routine patrol saw a light in a newly constructed house in Salek Gardens where no one was supposed to live yet. The door was unlocked, so she went in and discovered the corpse of a human. There was no obvious cause of death, but due to the circumstances, it is highly suspicious and murder is suspected." Raithan smiled at me. "That's the gist of it. We can go into details on location."

A human murder victim. "Does that fall under fatality, or are you in interspecies affairs?" I asked.

"I thought I told you I am not in the peace corps," Raithan said and slowed down the groundwheeler. We had reached a part of the city where new, fashionable buildings were constantly under construction. Salek Gardens must be close by. "Will a short walk be all right for you?" he added.

At least it appeared to be a general question and not spurred by his noticing how rough a morning I'd had. I suspect I am not the only person with a disability or chronic illness who is perpetually caught between gratitude and annoyance when others take their condition into consideration. "Walking is fine," I replied.

"Good. I want to get a feel for the area." Raithan halted the vehicle, rotated all six wheels and slid smoothly into the space between two other groundwheelers at the side of the street.

It was a cool and foggy Nantheam morning, and the dampness did no wonders for my breathing. I touched the inhaler in my pocket out of habit. This weather would not have bothered me much before my time on Almaimak, and I was hoping that the worsening of my respiratory dysfunction was only temporary.

I tried to come up with a topic to smalltalk about, but when I glanced up at Raithan's profile, his expression was more closed and serious than I had ever seen. For a moment I was self-absorbed enough to wonder if I had said or done something wrong to warrant such a drastic change of mood. And then I recalled we were on our way to a murder scene and felt quite embarrassed for even considering that his mind was intent on any other matter.

Raithan stopped, turned around and took a couple of stills of our surroundings with his patch. Then he continued without a word, and I followed.

I saw nothing remarkable. A few groundwheelers passed by, a lone pedestrian too preoccupied with their own patch to notice us or anything else almost collided with a street light and hurriedly looked around to make sure no one had seen it. Apart from that, we were alone in the street, which made sense because the buildings here were still largely unoccupied. No one except work crews and people taking a short cut through Salek Gardens would have a reason to be here.

Raithan stopped once more and snapped a few stills. I had no idea of what. He quickly moved on again.

The neighborhood was clean and modern and a little too sterile for anything outside of a lab, lacking the charm and personality of older districts like Monarth Park or Deith. The streets were straight and broad and the buildings nestled behind front gardens that were unremarkable at the moment but for the flowerbeds with, unsurprisingly, salek flowers, outlining them. They would no doubt grow into beautiful little oases once the houses all became occupied and their owners put effort into them.

Raithan slipped on a pair of forensic gloves, bent down, reached his hand far into one of the flowerbeds and, to my astonishment, retrieved a patch. "Well, then," he said. "What does this tell you, Kellieth?"

"That someone dropped their patch," I suggested, "and haven't found it because it was hidden by the plants?"

Raithan smiled. "Rather a lot more than that. This patch is almost brand new. It is of a human brand and design and belongs to someone large-boned." He demonstrated this last part by holding the ends of the strap together, creating a circumference that would fit both of my wrists. "It was thrown away intentionally, which you can tell from the distance into the flowerbed where I found it."

"I see," I said. "So do you think it is connected to the murder?"

"Oh yes." He slipped the patch into a small sealable bag, put it in his pocket and removed the forensic gloves again. "And we will soon discover what."

We continued for a little while before my companion stopped once more, this time to look at the house behind one of those bland front gardens. A bright blue groundwheeler was parked a little haphazardly by the side of the road. It was the sort with big wheels and tires that provided traction in any environment, and it looked a little too bombastic to fit into a perfectly civilized Nantheam neighborhood.

"Here we are," Raithan announced. And then he bent down again and breathed in deeply. He took another few stills. "Stay behind me," he told me as he approached the house, still absorbed in studying the ground as we walked.

An access path ran next to the front garden from the street to the entrance of the house. It was soft and damp from a recent downpour, and there were several sets of footprints as well as visible groundwheeler tracks.

At the house, we were met by a man around my own unimpressive height but with considerably more muscle and skin as dark as Raithan's. His hair was only shoulder length and dyed a brown hue "Raithan!" he said. "Welcome back. I'm glad you could make it so quickly. Everything has been left untouched."

"No, it hasn't," replied Raithan, somewhat peevishly, pointing at the wet ground. "It looks like the entire criminal offense corps of Nantheam has enjoyed a picnic here."

"Well, everything at the actual crime scene," the man said.

Raithan motioned to the street we had come from. "I take it that's your groundwheeler parked there?"

"Yes. It's new, in fact. Why?"

Raithan didn't answer his question. "Second Class Investigator Greithon OenKelneinth," he said instead by way of introduction, "meet my friend, Doyen Kellieth ReinAraneinth."

I held out my hands and bent my head over them in greeting. "Pleased to meet you," I said.

"Likewise, I'm sure," Greithon said, quickly bowing over his upturned palms as well. "I'm sorry, Raithan, but they are your *friend*? I need documentation to verify that they're cleared to—"

Raithan's eyes narrowed. "Hold on, Greithon. Please remind me under whose jurisdiction this case is now."

"Yours, sir," Greithon said reluctantly. "I called you because you are the most efficient and least intolerable of your lot."

Raithan did not look offended. "Exactly," he said. "You automatically put me in charge of the case when you asked for my involvement. Which means that I am free to bring whomever I wish. Come on, Kellieth."

I shook my head as I followed Raithan into the house to indicate to Greithon that I was as much at a loss as he. Probably, in fact, even more. Greithon was from the peace corps and Raithan was not. What was he then? Did he work for a private investigation service? But that would not grant him authority over the peace corps. He couldn't possibly be a federal agent. Could he?

The entrance hall was spacious and I had the brief thought that this would be a much nicer place to live than my current lodgings, albeit one I would never be able to afford. I shut down that line of thought fast because this was not a vacant house inspection. It was the scene of a murder.

We entered what was probably meant to be the common room, a large, square space empty of furniture. Only one box was sitting in a corner with a lantern of the sort often used to illuminate construction sites on it.

A woman wearing a transparent facemask was leaning against the wall with two displays floating above her patch that she was clearly crosschecking. She was around Raithan's height with a cool grey skintone and red hair arranged into a practical braid that flowed down almost to the back of her knees. She looked up when we entered and swiped away the displays. Of course, she had not been able to smell us in advance through the mask. For once, it was not I who had my nose blocked regarding other people's presence longer than anyone else in the room.

"Raithan?" the woman said, clearly taken aback by his presence and not just, I sensed, because he had entered unsmelled. "I didn't realize you were back on duty."

"I was not," Raithan said. "But your colleague outside personally called me, and so now I am. I am taking over the case."

"I gathered as much. You don't do things by halves," the woman said. "As long as you're ready..."

Raithan did not continue this mysterious conversation. "First

Class Investigator Lystrath NefNenenth, Kellieth ReinAraneinth," he said instead. "They are here to give me a hand with the investigation."

"So you are his new assistant. Good luck with that," Lystrath told me sympathetically. Her name indicated she was of Synal descent, but her accent was that of a native Menal citizen of Nantheam.

I didn't know whether I should correct her assumption, so I merely smiled and turned my attention back to Raithan.

He was honing in on the centerpiece of the room which was, of course, the corpse. It lay on the floor and, disturbingly, something was written in sloppy, brown strokes on the wall next to it. There was a discarded scarf and a toppled over disposable cup close by, but Raithan only briefly beheld those two items.

The corpse's smell was that of a recently deceased mammal, and with how strong the tang was even to me, it was no wonder Lystrath wore a mask.

Raithan had, surprisingly, not put on a mask or even nose plugs. How he could stand it, I did not know.

I have worked on research projects with humans before and have always gotten along quite well with that species. Our fellow mammals have a poor sense of smell, which is probably for the best because they generally have strong odors. Their sweat, their breath, their perfumes and various beauty products and soaps are offensive to various degrees. Their food can be blatant and unrefined too, but sometimes they surprise by hitting the right notes perfectly. I have heard other wendek describe having a conversation with a human as being constantly shouted at because their smells and pheromones are so loud. Well, I suspect I, in turn, am less offensive to humans than the average wendek because I don't react strongly to all that.

"He isn't wearing a patch," Lystrath said.

"So I see," Raithan noted. But he had picked one up outside. One of a human brand. If that was the dead human's, why not mention it to Lystrath?

I swallowed and looked at the corpse. I was inclined to agree with

Lystrath that it was male, though I was not certain of this. He must have been one of the sad, pale beige humans in life, but now his skin was waxy and yellowish white. His brown eyes were open and staring at the ceiling. The hair on his head was so short I could easily make out his strange, rounded ears, but he had an astounding amount of facial hair. I had to remind myself that I had, in fact, worked with humans with beards before and that they were perfectly civilized. The corpse's clothes looked clean and of a fashionable cut. What really stood out to me was his posture and facial expression. His arms were spread out, his hands clenched, and his legs were drawn up and twisted as if he had suffered great pain as he died. His face was drawn in a mask of agony and something else... Hatred, perhaps. Or maybe it was the bared omnivore's pointed canines that made him look so fierce to people whose teeth were not meant to rip apart flesh.

The whole thing was overwhelming. I took a step back, away from the corpse, and a sharp intake of breath that resulted in a noseful of foul air.

"Are you all right?" Lystrath asked.

"Yes," I managed, fighting the urge to throw up. I have seen dead animals and even a couple of dead wendek before. But the latter had been cleaned up nicely. I have never seen a dead human. And never a corpse with such a ferocious odor.

"Is this your first murder case working with him?" Lystrath asked, still under the impression that I was Raithan's assistant.

"Yes," I said again.

"You should put on a mask," she said, resting a hand on my shoulder for comfort.

"They don't need one," Raithan said. I had no idea how someone with a sense of smell that must far surpass mine was able to stand this. He was crouching by the corpse and had been examining it while I was gawking and gagging. Now he looked over his shoulder at me. "Do you need to step outside, though?"

"No, I'm fine," I said.

"Then come here." Raithan held up something for me.

I swallowed and approached him, taking the pair of forensic gloves he was offering me. At least putting on such gloves for protection and to avoid contamination was professional second nature to me.

"The peace corps were partially right. There is no immediately obvious cause of death," Raithan said as I crouched next to him. "No wounds, and no broken bones. However... Please breathe, Kellieth."

"I am!" I hissed. I wasn't, really, and quickly took a deep breath.

"No, I meant for you to smell him. His mouth, in particular."

It did occur to me that I could get up, leave the house, and be done with this unpleasant business. But I was a scientist, and I wanted to know what Raithan did, didn't I? So I crouched next to him and sniffed.

"Oh," I said.

"So what do you think?"

"He was poisoned," I said. "He has been drinking black brew, but that's not the only smell. There's something else. Something sharper... If you want a qualified guess, I would say a compound hathnitrate." I glanced at the corpse's horrible, staring eyes. "It explains his tiny pupils and why it looks like he died in agony. It eats away at a person's insides rapidly if ingested in a concentrated dose. But it could be other poisons too. If I had a sample, I would be able to tell."

Raithan smiled. "Oh, you are good," he murmured. I would be lying if I said I hadn't been told the exact same thing in the exact same tone by a lover once or twice.

My companion stood up. As he did, a small object clattered across the floor. I did not see where it came from. Maybe it had been hidden in the folds of the dead human's clothes. Raithan snatched it up before it rolled away.

"What was that?" Lystrath asked.

Raithan examined the object. It was a ring. "Huh," he said.

"Well?" Lystrath insisted.

"Not the most condemning piece of evidence," Raithan said as he put the ring into a small, transparent bag like he had with the patch. "But I'll take it and have a closer look. All right," he added and turned to the writing on the wall that everybody had ignored so far. "This is obvious, but..."

"Yes," agreed Lystrath.

"Is it?" I asked. Because it made very little sense to me.

"Go ahead, then," Raithan told Lystrath in a friendly sort of manner.

She gestured to the brownish letters on the light blue wall. "Well, the murderer or the victim clearly painted it. It says 'Haenva', so I assume the writer was interrupted and meant to write the name Haenvaith. I'm sure that's the name of a person involved in this case, which confirms that it's an interspecies problem because Haenvaith is a Menal name. As for what it is written with... I'm not sure. Whatever is in that cup, I suppose. I noticed a faint smell of something bitter before I put on my mask, but it's clearly not blood."

"Kellieth, if you please," Raithan said.

I'm not sure if he recognized how awkward it felt to be asked to identify scents when I was literally the living person with the worst sense of smell in the room. But I dutifully picked up the cup and sniffed at the dried remains. "Black brew. And that same smell as on his mouth."

"I thought so," Raithan said smugly.

"Black brew?" Lystrath asked. "What is that even?"

Raithan gestured for me to explain.

"Black brew is a drink favored by humans. It is a common name for all approximations of a traditional beverage called coffee which is brewed not entirely unlike twa but which is based on a certain bean local to the human home planet, Earth. Since it is expensive in the human diaspora, they have invented black brew. Usually, it consists of..." I cleared my throat. "Of various things that aren't particularly relevant right now. If I had a sample, I might be able to tell where it was produced, and I would most definitely be able to see if there is any hathnitrate in it."

"All right," Raithan said and fished another transparent bag out of his pocket. "Go ahead."

I carefully put the disposable cup into the bag.

"I think that's all the evidence we can gain here. I need the contact info on the officer who found the body so I can interview her," Raithan said.

"She's a general conduct officer. I'll send over her information," Lystrath said.

"Thank you." Raithan looked around one last time. "Well, good day to you, Lystrath."

"Wait," Lystrath protested. "Is that it?"

"Indeed. You and Greithon can arrange for the body to be removed now. Feel free to identify the victim if you want to. I will let you know if I need your assistance. If nothing else, I will give you a heads-up when I am about to catch the murderer," Raithan said. "But for your information, the writing on the wall isn't meant to be a Menal name. Haenva is Draspaarg and means revenge."

"So the murder is a draever?" Lystrath exclaimed.

"Not necessarily. In fact, everything points toward it being another human," Raithan said. "But I will be in touch. Come on, Kellieth."

Chapter V
BREAKFAST AT DIOGENES

"Nothing like a fresh murder case in the morning," Raithan said as we were walking away from that fatal house in Salek Gardens. I must confess I was not certain it was a jest.

"Oh, come on," Raithan continued when he noticed my uncomfortable smell. "*I* didn't kill that human. But I have a feeling the whole affair isn't as politically complicated as the peace corps fears. Now that Greithon has handed over the case to me, however, I'll sort it out for the corps."

I chewed my lower lip. As curious and eager as I had been to know what my neighbor did, having witnessed it firsthand made me a little apprehensive. But some things had been cleared up. He was not in the peace corps, and his authority exceeded that of the two investigators whom we had met. "So, you are with the FWSA?" I asked.

"Well done!" Raithan told me. "I am indeed a first class independent agent of the Federal Wendek Security Agency. Are you hungry?"

So my neighbor was a lot more than the highly intelligent and eccentric fellow I had expected him to be. If memory served me right, a first class independent agent was the highest rank given to a field agent. "Um, a bit," I admitted, a little surprised at the sudden change of topic. But I hadn't managed to get breakfast before he whisked me away.

"Good. I'm so glad to hear that," he said.

"Why?" I asked.

Raithan bared his teeth in a startling grin. It made him look like one of the predatory species we share our galaxy with. "Well, first of all, I thought for a moment you were going to be sick in there, so it's nice to see you bounce back. Secondly, I need to do a bit of work before we pay the general conduct officer a visit, and I might as well do it over breakfast. Do you have any suggestions? The Agency will pay."

We got back into his groundwheeler while I considered the options. When I woke up that morning, having a meal sponsored by a powerful federal institution had not been on my agenda. "I don't go out so much anymore," I said. "But I used to frequent to a human-style eatery... Which may be in poor taste right now."

"Not at all. I think it's fitting, in fact," Raithan said.

I directed him to what I was already thinking of as my old haunt, although it had been only a half month since I last visited Diogenes. Incidentally, it was the day when the hyperdrive was set in motion for moving into the same building as Raithan.

"How quaint," my companion remarked as we entered the establishment.

Being here with Raithan made my nose, as the saying goes, pick up on things I had taken for granted before. The interior was colorful in a way that seemed just slightly off. You know how white is associated with cold, utmost formality and aloofness and light yellow and beige are more soothing. Or how silver is considered bland rather than exclusive. There were absolutely no yellow or beige surfaces here, but an abundance of white and silver accents. I always assumed this is befitting for a human eatery, but Raithan's gaze around the place made me want to explain or defend the choice.

And then there were the smells. Black brew was easy to pick out, but nearly as clear was something unidentifiable that must be a protein based substance that mimicked the smell of actual animal meat being cooked. While they thankfully do not anymore, humans used to eat other mammals as well as fish and birds.

"Is Diogenes the name of a dish or a cuisine?" Raithan asked, undoubtedly picking up on a lot more smells than I. Perhaps this place appeared too crude and vulgar for him, I thought. But he did not appear to take offense.

"No," I said, "it's the name of a famous human philosopher from what I believe is an allegorical work." No need to elaborate on the nonsensical nature of that story.

"Will you order?" Raithan asked as we sat down at an empty table in the back of the eatery. I was trying to get us as far away from the kitchen as possible.

"Certainly. What do you want? They have a menu on their VoidSpace with explanations if you aren't used to human food," I said.

Raithan leaned back and stretched like a lazy syraxh. "I trust you to pick. My fate," he intoned, "is in your hands, Kellieth."

"Funny, I rather feel as if it's the exact opposite," I murmured. If he heard me, he did not show it. I ordered a strong cup of black brew for myself, a cup of tea for Raithan and a simple, hearty breakfast that had an appropriate amount of proteins, without mimicking meat, to keep us satisfied for a while.

Raithan pulled up a display from his patch and made it opaque so neither I, nor anyone else on the opposite side of it, could see what he was doing. Then he placed the patch he had picked from the flowerbed on the table.

"I couldn't help noticing you did not tell First Class Investigator Lystrath about that," I said, indicating the patch.

"I did not."

"But it is none of my business?"

He blinked as if he was only now registering that I was making an inquiry. "Oh," he said, "I know those two investigators. They will try to help with this case and try to outperform each other no matter what I say. So I gave Lystrath enough to keep both of them occupied scrabbling for clues and evidence and out of my way. I will let them have the patch after I have examined it."

"I see." In truth, I was not sure I did. I had stumbled into an established working relationship involving the two peace corps investigators and my federal agent neighbor without knowing their history at all.

Raithan returned his attention to his work. I doubt he even tasted the meal. I for my part checked up on the news. Indeed, there was a story about the peace corps finding a human body in an otherwise empty house, but there were fewer details than I already knew.

"Huh," Raithan said after a while.

"Yes?" I encouraged, expecting him to explain the results of his research.

"Is there supposed to be plant residue at the bottom of my cup?" he asked, tipping the vessel to show me.

"Yes, it happens. Those are tea leaves."

"Do you have leaves in your cup too?"

"No, because I am having black brew," I said patiently. "It is not brewed on leaves." Still, there was some sludge at the bottom of my cup.

"It's good to know I have a human expert with me," he said. "This is turning out to be a study in black brew."

"I'm hardly an expert," I said, fidgeting with the cup. "Anyway, have you been able to make any theories so far?"

Raithan actually laughed at this. "Haven't you?"

"I'm not the FWSA agent here," I countered, "and I don't know what you've been working on so far."

"No, but we were both at the scene of the crime. I think I have a fairly good idea of what transpired last night."

"I am sure you do," I told him. "Because you have experience with this sort of thing whereas I'm just the neighbor you dragged along to a crime scene.

"Oh, Kellieth, you are far more than just a neighbor," Raithan said, which I had no idea how to react to. "And I will tell you what happened. But not here." He rose and sauntered up to the counter to pay for our breakfast.

"All right," Raithan said when we were back in his groundwheeler and on our way to the address of the general conduct officer. "The victim arrived by rent ride at the empty house along with his killer. Despite the Draspaarg on the wall and Greithon's panic about this being a complicated, political interspecies affair, which is why he called me, the killer was human too. Taller than the victim and a great deal less wealthy. Around your height, Kellieth, which makes me think they've got a male physique, but I won't pretend to know how they identify. The victim was intoxicated and had to be coerced to come along, but he did not struggle a great deal. The killer brought the lamp that we found, gave their victim a cup of black brew laced with poison, and I am certain it was all premeditated."

"You figured all that out from examining the victim's patch?" I asked. That was impressive.

"What? No," Raithan said, "that's what I observed at the crime scene. I haven't told you anything relating to the patch yet."

"But hang on," I interrupted. "I don't get it. I know the black brew was contaminated with a poisonous substance, and it makes sense that the killer brought the lamp and had planned the murder because people rarely run around with poison on them, but... the rest?"

"All right," my companion said, slowing down his groundwheeler as the traffic was beginning to get heavy. "These days, investigators rely a lot on digital footprints, but sometimes you have to look at actual footprints too. We tend to forget that evidence can come in other shapes than surveillance clips and patch security violation. And when it comes to the physical world, we tend to rely a little too much on our noses. However, since it rained last night, it was easy to make out the marks from the rent ride's wheels in the mud leading up to the house. As you probably know, rent rides tend to be wider than private vehicles. There were two sets of footprints going in, one of them stumbling a few times and zig-zagging a little, which is why I believe he was intoxicated. Only one set came back. The stride length usually corresponds with the height of a person for both wendek and humans. The killer's match yours. And also, did you notice the writing on the wall was at your eye height? That's an indication as well."

"All right, but the financial situation of the two?" I asked. I was half convinced he was making up these things.

"The footprints again. The soles of our victim's shoes' are new and have a clear pattern. The other person's prints were worn uneven, and there was a small piece of repair film left in one of their indentations on the ground. Also, the killer would not have left the scarf if it were theirs, and it was of an expensive brand."

I absorbed this. "Well, when you put it like that, it doesn't seem like magic at all," I said.

"My deductions couldn't be further from magic," Raithan told me. "Now, do you have any other questions?"

"Do you usually work alone?" I asked.

This paused him. "I— Well, yes, these days I do. Why?"

I smiled. "I deducted it from your eagerness in explaining your methods."

Raithan laughed again. "Well done."

I thought that perhaps he was disposed to answer a few more personal questions at this point. "Both investigators implied that you have been away for a while," I noted.

"Yes, they did," Raithan said without missing a beat. "But right now we are discussing the case."

Well, then. All my modest powers of deduction told me was that he was not going to lie to me. But I could not help wondering. If he had only been on a vacation or taken time off while he was moving, there was hardly any reason to skirt the question.

I cleared my throat and returned my attention to the case. "All right... So now you only have to answer what happened to the driver and why, if the killer is human and not draever, they would write in Draspaarg. Actually, I don't get why they would write anything at all. What about fingerprints and DNA? And above all else... Why did they want to kill the victim in the first place? It takes a lot to make someone murder another person."

"Bravo! You sum up the difficulties of the situation succinctly and well," Raithan said as if I'd passed some kind of test. "The killer was wearing gloves, another proof that it was premeditated, by the way. They wrote the message to throw off the peace corps, probably. I'm not a specieist, but it is a very draever-like thing to do."

"Since you know so much, what about the identity of the victim? And the killer?"

Raithan tapped the air with two fingers. "Now we are getting to the patch. It was not difficult to break through its security. According to the personal information on it, our victim is one Enoch Drebber. He arrived on Ganmak two months ago on a business trip with his secretary, Johanna Stangerson."

"Am I imagining things, or are there quotation marks around business and secretary?" I asked.

"Astute," Raithan acknowledged. "I don't know the killer's name, but I found out a few more things from the patch, of course. Nonetheless, we are almost at our destination."

"How convenient." My neighbor apparently enjoyed impressing me with his skills, but he also wanted to keep some of the results of his work to himself for now, possibly because he wanted to present them in a dramatic fashion at the right moment, I thought.

CHAPTER VI
WHAT VANTHEIN SEINKEIWANNEINTH HAD TO TELL

Our next destination was Athlei Court, a briefly fancy part of Nantheam. If our own neighborhood was old-fashioned, it was so in a way that gave it charm and quaint personality. This part of our homeworld's greatest city was much newer and home to a mashup of different styles of architecture. If you thought it looked like a bunch of craftspeople and architects had been tasked with creating a building each that had then been erected quickly and without much thought for quality in building materials, you would be absolutely right. It was done as part of a competition some 20 years back, and because the buildings were supposed to be works of art, they were allowed to stay.

In Athlei Court, one finds almost gravity defying spires looming at an angle next to rounded housings that supposedly reflect our civilization's earliest extra-planetary settlements, and buildings that consist almost entirely of colored glass panes because someone, apparently, decided that if a thing is aesthetically pleasing, having more of it would necessarily be better.

The buildings were, however, not in the best state at this point because any interest of novelty they had enjoyed was far gone, and they had become relatively cheap and somewhat frowned upon by the elite they had originally been meant to house.

The officer lived in a building that looked fairly normal but for the roof's many angled surfaces that could not possibly be a more efficient way of doing photovoltaic panels than the normal larger panes.

We approached the house, and Raithan smiled at the little camera above the front door when a voice asked us to state our business.

"Ah, General Conduct Officer Vanthein SeinkeiWanneinth," he said. "I am Raithan WeinZalneinth, First Class Independent Agent of the FWSA, and this is my intern, Kellieth ReinAraneinth. We have some questions about your round last night. Do you mind if we come in?"

"ID?" the voice asked.

Raithan reached into his jacket and retrieved a small metal disc. He quickly traced a pattern on it and held it up as a projection appeared, rotating slowly. One side showed the logo of the FWSA, and the other had Raithan's name, rank and still. I had seen these identifiers often enough in entertainment, but never in real life. "You are welcome to scan it properly, but I doubt this camera can do that," he said.

"I already reported everything to the peace corps. I talked to the investigators, Lystrath and Greithon," the voice said.

"We know. The case was passed on to me, and so I require your cooperation." If there was a hint of threat in Raithan's voice, his smile made up for it.

"All right. Come in," the voice sighed, and the door swung open.

"Intern, though?" I said as we waited for the elevator.

"If she needs to see ID to let me in, I don't think she would be happy to accept anyone who isn't employed by the the peace corps or the FWSA," said Raithan.

"You could at least have said I'm your assistant or something."

"Would you like that?" he asked.

"Well, it sounds better."

Vanthein SeinkeiWanneinth opened the door of her apartment and glared at both of us. Given the fact that she worked night shifts, she probably slept at this time of the day. Her attire looked hastily assembled and her hair was a loose, yellow mess. "Come on in, then," she said. She led us to the living area of her home and did not ask us if we wanted something to drink or even to sit down. "What does the FWSA want from me?"

Raithan, paying back the officer's lack of courtesy with his own, took a seat on a couch. I ignored his glance at me and kept standing. "All we want is to hear what happened in your own words," he said.

Vanthein sat down on the edge of a couch opposite Raithan's, and her nostrils flared, double-checking his intentions. "All right," she said. "My patrol was routine. It started at midnight, and I was riding my slider slowly to keep an eye on things. It was a quiet night, probably on account of it being damp, and it began to rain an hour into my shift. I headed to Salek Gardens after greeting a fellow officer on their way home from a shift. You can check with them if you doubt me."

"That won't be necessary," my companion said and waved her on.

"So anyway, it was dark and wet and lonely out, and then a light in one of the houses caught my eye. It surprised me because that whole street is still empty. They barely finished building the houses there. So I thought to myself I'd go see if one of the work crews had left a light on or if someone had broken in. Squatters, maybe. One of those draever gangs you hear about on the news. Or humans. You know how they are with other people's property."

I wanted to protest at the eagerness to blame another species, but Raithan must have sensed it because he looked sharply at me in a way that made me clamp my mouth shut.

"So anyway, I got to the door..."

"Yes, and then you got off your slider and walked back to the street. May I ask why?" Raithan said.

Vanthein jerked back. "How do you know that?"

"The slider tracks went almost up to the door, but I saw your footprints too. Go on, please."

"Right. Okay. Yes, I thought maybe I had missed something. But I didn't see anything, and the street was still empty. I went back to the door and it was ajar, so I pushed it open and went in. I drew my dart gun at this point, but you probably already know that somehow."

"I didn't, but it stands to reason," Raithan said.

"I continued to the room where I'd seen the light, and there was the lamp. And that's when I saw the dead human."

"And I take it you didn't touch anything? Pick up the lamp? Move the body?"

Vanthein scoffed. "Look here, I might not be a fancy federal agent like you, but I know how to handle a potential crime scene. I did touch the body to check for breath and a pulse, but he was quite dead. Not for long, though."

"He came back to life?" Raithan asked, and I knew him well enough by now to catch his deadpan tone.

"What? No!" Vanthein exclaimed. "Oh, for the Creators' sakes. Are you even taking this seriously?"

"I assure you," Raithan said, all hints of amusement gone now, "that I am taking it very seriously. So please go on."

Vanthein breathed out in annoyance. "So I called the criminal offense corps, and an investigator named Greithon arrived soon after. I went home after handing over the case because my shift was done by then."

"And was the street empty at that point?"

"It was very early morning in an area where no one lives yet, so yes. Though I did almost collide with a person when I emerged from access path by the front garden."

"Really? How so?" Raithan asked, leaning forward as if he was trying to detect the other person's scent on her.

"They were intoxicated. Might have been vapor, but they stank like nobody's business too."

"Can you describe the person?"

"Not very tall," Vanthein said, making a gesture toward me. "Around your intern's height, probably. They were wearing an opaque facemask and a hat, so it was kind of hard to see them properly in the dark. Their coat was dark grey."

"And what happened to this person?" Raithan asked.

"I told them to go home and sleep it off." Vanthein scoffed. "Not much else to do. I did ask if they needed help, and they said they were fine."

Raithan actually groaned. "All right. That's all I need from you then, officer Vanthein. Thank you for your cooperation. I think we are all safe with you out there in the general conduct corps."

Vanthein's face lit up in a smile for the first time. "Thank you."

"Because if you were in the criminal offense corps, Nantheam would overflow with criminals. Come on, Kellieth."

I bowed to Vanthein and tried to smile apologetically on the way out as I followed Raithan.

"What the thak was that for?" I asked, crestfallen, when we out of earshot.

Raithan turned to me. "That absolute dimdek!" he said. "She had our murderer right there and did nothing!"

I laughed. "Oh, come on! Is this because they were the right height? What kind of criminal would come back to the scene of the crime like that?"

"They came back for the ring!" Raithan sighed. "Oh well. We can still use that little piece of evidence to our advantage. I think I know exactly how. But right now, let's get you home."

"Wait, what about the black brew sample?" I protested. "Don't you want to verify what kind of poison was used?"

Raithan breathed in sharply as he studied me. "I don't think we need to spend your energy on that right now. I got what I need from Enoch Drebber's patch," he said. "If it can be of help later, we can examine the cup. As long as the evidence bag is sealed, it will stay wet."

"But—" I swallowed. I hadn't realized how much I wanted to do the analysis until that moment. My motivations were easily identifiable. First of all, I wanted to show Raithan that I was useful. I wanted to contribute meaningfully to the case he had dragged me into. Secondly, I longed to be in a lab. I longed to dive into research and analyses and do what I was good at.

"Kellieth," Raithan cut through my thoughts, "You are exhausted." He was looking at me with the closest thing to worry I had so far seen on his face.

I was about to protest, but all of a sudden, fatigue was creeping up on me fast. Truth be told, I had been so invested in Raithan's work that I had hardly considered my own health and needs all morning. It stung that such mild exertions should have such an effect on me, but I knew he was right. "All right," I conceded.

CHAPTER VII
AN UNEXPECTED INTRUSION

It was not until I had bidden Raithan goodbye and beheld my own face in the mirror in my apartment that I understood why my neighbor was worried. Apart from feeling fatigued, I was pale and looked like I was on the brink of collapse. Once upon a time, when I was a student, I could stay up all night working on a thesis or an experiment. Even as a fully fledged doyen, I would work all day and well into the night if I had to, pausing only to eat and get a bit of exercise. But gone was that energetic, young chemist. My breathing was not bothering me more than it usually did when the air was humid these days, but after a restless night and a morning of considerable excitement, I was utterly spent. I knew I should not be surprised. There was a reason I was living off a pension right now and not pursuing an active career. But still.

I gracelessly kicked off my shoes, shrugged out of my jacket and went straight to bed.

I only intended to rest for a little while, but I fell asleep almost immediately. Yet, I would be lying if I said the quality of my nap was particularly good. I dreamed of distorted, human faces staring up at me. Of corpses grasping at my ankles as I walked around them. Of the smell of death so strong I gagged. And of, which was completely random, one of my colleagues back on Almaimak asking me if I had found a date for the ball at the castle. I have no idea what that was about. Not all dreams are easily decipherable, and sometimes they are really nothing more than our brains keeping themselves entertained while we sleep.

I woke up an hour later and, needing a break from subconscious absurdities and horrors, decided to make a cup of black brew. Its bitter smell was comforting, and I shuffled into my living room and curled up on my couch under a blanket.

While I was sipping the fortifying beverage, my thoughts returned to the events of the morning. I had wanted to know more about Raithan. I had tried to figure out what he did, and he had been as mysterious as he was handsome and infuriating. I had entertained the idea that he might be a peace corps officer. Fairly close, but not accurate.

Analyzing our interactions and everything he had not said, it made sense that Raithan was an FWSA agent. What was truly puzzling was the fact that he had showed up at my door on a perfectly ordinary morning and invited me to come with him to a crime scene without any preamble. That he had shared details about the case with me and brought me along to interview a peace corps officer. As little as I knew about how the Federal Wendek Security Agency worked, I found it hard to believe that its agents were allowed to do that for all that first class independent agents might have certain privileges... My mind also kept meandering back to Greithon and Lystrath. To how they treated Raithan, and to how it was implied that he had been away for a while.

And then there was the case itself. How had Enoch Drebber ended up poisoned in that house? Where had his secretary gone? What was the motive for the murder? And what else did Raithan know that I could not fathom?

I reached no conclusions. My brain still felt sluggish, and I allowed myself to drift off again.

I started awake an indeterminable while later. My apartment was dark now and the remainder of my black brew cold. And I instantly knew I was not alone.

I slid off the couch as noiselessly as I could and crouched behind the small table next to it. I was indifferent to most of the furnishings the apartment came with, but a few items I positively disliked. One of those was the lamp I now curled my fingers around. It was a heavy, opulent thing and looked like a bad pastiche of some older design. And it would do well as an improvised weapon against an intruder.

The floor creaked somewhere near the door, giving me a hint as to the location of the other person. Someone with a normally functioning sense of smell would have picked up on the intentions of the intruder and, if they knew them, their identity. Undoubtedly, the other person had a rough idea where I was right now as well as my present state of mind. I have on occasion gotten into trouble on account of my hyposmia, and it is these experiences caused by my disadvantage that have led me to be very cautious indeed.

My position was not ideal, but when the intruder came closer, I would be able to leap up and aim a swing of the ugly lamp at their kneecaps or thrust it at their groin, causing the maximum amount of incapacitation without overstepping the boundaries of reasonable self-defense. I adjusted my grip on my unorthodox weapon.

The footfalls stopped. Then resumed toward my location. I had to act now. I came up in front of the intruder, lunging at them with the lamp, but they sidestepped my blow more nimbly than anyone ought to and—

"Kellieth! It's me!" exclaimed a familiar voice.

I had the lamp raised over my head now, ready to strike again, but in the dim light, I could make out my neighbor's face, and I finally picked up on his scent too. "Raithan," I gasped.

"If I could dissuade you from trying to bludgeon me to death, perhaps that horrible piece of furnishing could shed some light on the situation instead."

I lowered my makeshift weapon. How dare he sneak up on me like that and have the audacity to make such nonchalant puns on top of everything! I put the lamp down and turned it on. "How did you get in?"

"The door on your side of the common room was unlocked," Raithan said. "Are you all right? I didn't startle you too badly, did I?"

"You could have knocked!" I said.

"I did, but you did not reply, and I got... worried."

"You could have sent me a dispatch!"

"Check your patch."

I glanced down. Oh. He had. "You still sneaked up on me while I was asleep!" I said.

"And I'm sorry for that. Oh, but you surprise me, Kellieth. I had not expected your reaction to be quite that..."

"Violent?" I suggested.

"I was going to say reasonable. Anyway, you don't look very rested for someone who has presumably slept for hours. Is this morning's affair troubling you?"

"A bit," I admitted. "I can't stop trying to work out what happened in that house."

Raithan made an affirmative gesture. "Have you looked at any newsfeeds this afternoon?"

"No. Should I?"

"There is nothing in them that you and I don't already know. In fact, there is a great deal less. But no one mentions the ring I took at the crime scene, which is exactly what I wanted."

"Why?" I yawned.

"Because I am convinced the killer wants that ring. So," Raithan said, "I did this." He swiped at his patch, and mine lit up with a notification.

It was a lost property ad with a still attached that had been published on Nantheam's most popular social network-slash-signpost, The Sparkle.

I read the notice. Then stared up at Raithan in utter disbelief. "You put this on The Sparkle using my account?" I had not used it to reconnect with old acquaintances after returning to Ganmak since I knew very few who lived in Nantheam. And my sense of academic and personal defeat had prevented me from sending a jolly message or log in to make cheerful updates with stills of my own smiling, albeit more gaunt than usually, face.

"Yes. You don't mind, do you? I needed it to be inconspicuous."

"I kind of feel," I said, determined to stand my ground a little longer, "that there should be some kind of proper, federal procedure for things like this."

Raithan smiled. "I can't very well put the address of the Agency in the ad. The killer wouldn't come forward then."

I sighed. While that made sense, there still must be a normal procedure that did not involve federal agents arbitrarily using their unsuspecting neighbors' social media accounts. It was the sort of thing you might expect from a period drama, not actual, professional investigation. "Please don't do things like that without asking me first," I said.

"Does that mean you would not be adverse to my using your identity for investigational purposes in the future if only I ask you first?" Raithan asked.

I tilted my head back. "I never said that! But... Done is done, I suppose." Why could I not stay angry with him? It was not fair. "So what happens now?"

"Now," Raithan said, "we'll wait. I'll stay here so you aren't alone when they arrive."

"Yes because you have simply no way to quickly get from your apartment to mine," I intoned. "What makes you think anyone will even react to that ad? Why do you think the killer wants the ring? Also, I don't have one to give them."

"Oh yes, you have. I did not wait around idly while you slept. I had a ring printed for the purpose," he said, retrieving one from his pocket and holding it out to me. It did look very much like I remembered the ring from the crime scene. "Did you know that humans traditionally give a ring as a symbol of their love when they ask another human to become their lifelong partner?"

"Oh, Raithan. You shouldn't have," I told him because that was really the only way I could conceivably react to something as embarrassingly and blatantly flirtatious as that.

Raithan laughed. "As for whether anyone will react to the ad, I am confident our killer will be looking for that ring. It is important to them."

"Maybe, but if I were a murderer who lost something literally in the room where I killed a person, I would find it too risky to meet up with a stranger who claimed to have that item," I argued.

"And that is very reasonable of you. Yet, I believe the killer would risk almost anything sooner than losing that ring. They might send a friend to pick it up, but they do want it back very badly." Raithan began to pace back and forth in front of me, slowly, but purposefully. "I believe they dropped it while standing over the corpse and did not notice at the time. After leaving the house, they discovered it was gone and hurried back. The footprints near the access path indicated this. But at this point, Vanthein was already present because the killer had also neglected to take the lamp with them or to at least turn it off. Now, when Vanthein saw them, they did everything in their power to conceal their identity. They are tall enough to be a somewhat short wendek, and they were wearing a facemask and gloves too. They also smelled, as you will recall our not-so-bright general conduct officer mentioning, and I suspect they may have doused themself in perfume to throw others off the scent, as it were. Vanthein thought they were intoxicated, but that was probably a ploy too. Now, the killer was prevented from going back in, but they will keep an eye on the news to see if anyone mentions the ring being found at the crime scene. When that does not happen, they start entertaining the idea that perhaps they did not lose it in the house, after all. Perhaps they lost it somewhere else in the area."

"In the rent ride?" I suggested.

Raithan wagged a finger at me. "Good theory, but no. They have no idea where it was lost, but they do know for certain that it was not in the rent ride. Still, they are desperate to find it. So of course they check for PlaNet advertisements, including the lost property section of The Sparkle. And there, they will come across one Kellieth ReinAraneinth who kindly has posted a message about finding a ring in the street and a still of it."

I did not understand why Raithan was so certain the culprit knew they had not lost the ring in the rent ride, but I accepted that he probably had a good reason. "All right," I said. "And then what?"

"Then we wait for someone to respond and subsequently show up here." Raithan looked around my living room. "I don't suppose you have any arms?"

"You mean apart from these two?" I said, holding up said limbs.

Raithan blinked, then grinned. "Yes, apart from those attached to your body, and that lamp."

"I have a shocker for self-defense. Do you expect I will need it?" I continued, more soberly. Like I mentioned, I am used to taking precautions. I have some experience with other weapons, but there was no need to tell him that, especially because I was not in possession of a license for anything but a shocker.

"Well, our killer is desperate, so it is best to be prepared. Please get it so you are equipped for every eventuality. However, I doubt you will need it. I will be here with you."

I sized him up. "And you are hiding a weapon somewhere on your person right now, I suppose?"

Raithan reached behind him and into his sash and pulled out a sleek, black gun that somehow looked exactly like a thing he would own and possibly display on a shelf in his apartment if he didn't mind advertising his profession.

Chapter VIII
OUR AD BRINGS A VISITOR

While Raithan concealed his own weapon again, I went to get my shocker from my bedroom. It was a handy little thing that fit effortlessly into a pocket.

As I was returning, my patch let me know I had a Sparkle message. "It's a reply to your ad," I told Raithan. "The spark is from someone with a private profile." I showed him the message. *Thank you for keeping the ring. Can I drop by to pick it up tonight?*

"Very good," Raithan said. "Don't reply immediately." He brought up a display from his own patch and quickly typed something. Then breathed out in annoyance. "Avoiding detection by my Irregulars. Oh well, it was worth a try."

"Your what now?" I asked.

"My Irregulars. They're clever little programs disguised as ad bots that I use for discreet digital surveillance. I set them up to see if they could pinpoint the sender, but apparently this is not someone as lax with digital security as you," Raithan explained.

I decided to ignore that comment.

"Give them your address and tell them you are home for the rest of the day," he continued.

I did.

Thank you. I will be there in an hour, said the reply. There was no still of the respondent available to the public, but the name and pronouns were those of a human woman.

"So now we wait," Raithan said. "And to keep us occupied, I know exactly what we should do."

"And that is?"

"I am going to take care of your security problem."

"My only security problem is a certain federal agent," I quipped.

"I'm not an expert. If I can get into your account, so can anyone else," Raithan argued.

I very much doubted that. Nevertheless, I was interested in discovering precisely how he broke into my Sparkle account. It turned out that he had pretended to be me attempting to access my account from a new device and taken advantage of my lack of both patch and social media security to do so. As he explained it to me, Raithan also fixed the problem by setting up a couple of verification measurements that would be cumbersome if I wanted to connect another device to my account at some point, but reasonable enough.

Time crept along and eventually, someone triggered the building's front door's sensor.

"Act inconspicuously," Raithan instructed me as I made my way to the door. "I will take action if any is needed."

The person on the screen looked nothing like I expected the killer to. She was human, all right, but it was an old-looking person who peered into the camera.

"Yes?" I said in Standard.

"Are you Kellieth ReinAraneinth?" asked the human, butchering the diphthongs in my name and making it sound like Kellis RainArnainth.

"Yes, I am," I said.

"I'm here about your ad on The Sparkle," the human said in clearly accented Standard, but I am no linguist and could not tell where that accent belonged.

"Oh, right. Come on in," I said and unlocked the front door, then opened the door to my apartment.

I knew all about the discomfort climbing the stairs outside can produce in a person, but if the woman's wince was anything to go by, she was suffering from joint pains and not any respiratory difficulties. However, the moment she entered my apartment, I was in danger of getting those. She smelled human, of course, but on top of that was a layer of sickly sweet perfume that made my tongue feel swollen and threatened to make my eyes water.

"Come right in," I said, suppressing my body's urge to gag. "Would you like something to drink? I have— twa and water." I could have kicked myself for almost saying black brew. This person was either the murderer or was involved with what Raithan jokingly called a study in black brew.

"Thank you, but I am just here for the ring," the human woman said. She was a good deal shorter than I and wore a dress in a light orange color that would look great on a person with grey skin but clashed horribly with hers. The fabric strained around her chest and middle, for she was not a slight person even by human standards.

I showed her into the living room where Raithan was idly playing a puzzle game on his patch. He looked up, and there was something in his expression I couldn't quite place. Frustration? Discomfort? Oh, of course. If I was this affected by the smell, he must be extremely uncomfortable. "If you don't mind, I'd like to verify that the ring in question does belong to you," I said.

"Yes, of course. I would be lying if I said it did, but I am here on behalf of my daughter. It is her engagement ring," the woman said. "She was so upset to lose it and cried with relief when she saw your ad. Only, she is working tonight, so she sent me to get it for her. She would have taken time off to do it herself, but you know how it is. Trying to get by and support her old mother on a foreign planet and everything. Making ends meet can be difficult. But that ring means the world to her."

"Right," I said. "Do you, um, maybe have any stills of her wearing it?"

"Oh yes." The old lady pulled up a display from her patch and leaned close to me so I could get a good look. "Look, there she is," she said with warmth in her voice. Her perfume was making it hard to smell anything else.

The still was of a young, human woman. I honestly couldn't tell if there was a familial resemblance, but they had approximately the same pale pink skin tone. The young woman was smiling with her teeth exposed, looking directly at the camera and holding up a glass with a long stem.

She was not centered in the image but standing too far to the left for an aesthetically pleasing composition. And someone else stood next to her. I could make out the shoulder and side of that person. Someone taller than her and with a pinkish beige and fleshy hand sticking out of a black sleeve. Had this person been deliberately cut out of the still? Surely, there must be better ways to do that if they were a stranger who happened to get in the way.

I attempted to figure out where it had been taken. There was some furniture in the background that did not look like any wendek style I know. It was probably human.

The odorous, old woman magnified the subject's hand, and indeed a ring adorned one of her stubby fingers. It looked identical to both the one from the crime scene and the copy Raithan had given me.

"Can I see?" asked Raithan lightly and approached us. He put his arm around my shoulder. "Engagement ring, huh? Human traditions are so exciting. Right, Kelli?"

"Err," I said because between Raithan's smiling suggestively at me and squeezing my shoulder and the old human's sickening smell, I was fresh out of intelligent contributions to the conversation. I pulled away from them both. "Is this the ring, then?" I asked, producing the copy to show the human.

"Yes, that is it!" she exclaimed. "Oh, thank you so much. My daughter will be so happy now! She was devastated to think she had lost it."

"Where did you say she lost it, again?" Raithan asked. His

restraint was really remarkable. Somehow the artificial sweetness was worse than the natural stench of human decay I had witnessed at the scene of the murder.

"She thinks she lost it on her way home from work last night. See, she works at a restaurant in Werrin Gardens, and we live near Athlei Court, so it's only a short walk."

I glanced at Raithan, and he raised his hand to indicate to me that he needed nothing else.

"All right. Here you go," I said and held out the ring to her. "I am glad I was able to help you and your daughter."

The old human took the ring, admired for a moment and then stuffed it into her pocket. "Thank you so very much," she said. "My daughter will be so relieved. I really should give you a reward for finding it, but..."

"No need," I said. "It's the least I could do."

She bobbed her head in the human affirmative. "Well, thank you again."

I saw her to the door where she thanked me once more and then shuffled away. I closed the door and took a long, deep breath. The air was still foul with her smell. "All right," I said, returning to the living room. "Should we—" I paused, for Raithan was nowhere to be seen.

I heard a distinct retching sound from my toilet. Apparently, my neighbor was more affected by the smell than he let on. I went to open as many windows as possible to get rid of the stench. Most people had at least one censer, and in a fancier, newer apartment, there would be an air purifier installed in every room, but I was in possession of none of these things. It had not bothered me until this moment.

A few minutes later, Raithan appeared in the doorway. "Sorry about that," he said. "I should have taken precautions."

A mask or nose plugs, I assumed. "It's fine. Are you better now?" I asked. A tiny part of me found it reassuring that he was not supernaturally immune to strong odors.

"Yes. Ah, fresh air," he added and went to the nearest window where he stuck out his head and drew in a long breath.

"Do you think she was the murderer?" I asked.

"No," Raithan said, still relishing the fresh air.

"So she must be in league with our murderer, right? Should we follow her?" I ventured.

"We?" Raithan repeated, his familiar smugness returning to his handsome features.

"Or you. I meant you."

"She most definitely is an associate of the culprit, but there is no reason to follow," Raithan said. "There is a tracking device in that ring. We can discern her movements from here."

"That's clever. I didn't notice at all."

"It wouldn't have been very well hidden if you did," Raithan told me.

"Anyway, that was one horrible perfume. I have no idea how it got through Ganmak's customs," I said.

Raithan took one more gulp of the outside air and then turned to me. He was looking distinctly better now. "Maybe it didn't. Could someone make a perfume like that themself given the right ingredients?"

"Of course," I said. "Yes, they could. I could do that easily without having any prior experience making perfumes. Something that unrefined and repulsive would not be hard to put together. What I don't get is... Can humans really not smell how horrible that is?"

"I think that was entirely for our benefit. To throw us off any other scents, much like the person Vanthein met. I could barely tell if she was lying, though of course she was. But," he added and sat down on my couch and brought up a display from his patch. "Let's see where she is going."

We watched the tracking signal slowly move down our street.

"Did you notice the composition of that still?" I asked. "It looked like another person had been cut out."

"Indeed," Raithan agreed. "Very astute, my dear Doyen."

I had yet to decide whether he was making fun of me with this sort of statement.

The tracking signal turned right and stopped at an intersection. It crossed the street, went a little further and then stopped at another crossing near Jerril Park. And then the signal flickered and went out.

Raithan groaned and stood up.

"What?" I asked.

"She's more clever than she smelled," he said. "I'll be right back."

"Where are you... going?" I asked, but he had already run through my apartment and out of the door before I could even finish the sentence. "All right," I muttered and went to lock the door. "I'll wait for you, then."

It was almost an hour before my doorbell chimed. Not exactly what I'd call "be right back", but I rose and obediently opened the door. It was, of course, Raithan. He had gone out without a jacket and looked both cold and flushed as if he had been running.

"That was embarrassing," he panted as he flopped onto my couch. "Don't ever let the peace corps know. I have chaffed them so much that they would never let me hear the end of it."

"What happened?" I asked.

"Remember when I said we tend to rely too much on modern technology instead of looking for physical evidence?"

"Go on."

"Relying on a tracker was setting myself up for failure. I followed the signal to where it stopped. It was near a corner with a rainwater recycler. Our guest was gone. She must have deactivated the tracker by plunging the ring into the water barrel. Yet, I could still pick up her scent... Well, her stench, so I followed that across the street and around the whole thakking neighborhood. I lost the trail in Jerril Park. Or rather, I found the source of the scent." Raithan sighed dramatically. "She had dumped her clothes in a waste container."

"Hold on," I said, "You must have been right on her heels. She was at least half a meter shorter than you and old too. How could she disappear?"

"I very much doubt she was old," Raithan said. "I asked more than one passerby if they had seen an elderly human, but no one had. I'll wager that was a young person in good shape who had planned everything perfectly. She deactivated the tracker, ran to the park, dumped the perfumed outer layer of her clothes, and then disappeared among the people running or strolling in the park. She was probably wearing makeup that could be wiped off easily, too."

"That was clever," I said.

"And goes to show that our target has planned everything meticulously," Raithan said.

"So... What now?" I asked.

Raithan scrutinized me for a moment. "Now we get something to eat. It feels like a takeout sort of night, don't you think?"

I smiled. "Sure. What are you in the mood for?"

Raithan was already looking at his patch to find a suitable place to order from. "I could go for Lai cuisine. The spices will help get rid of the last of her odor too," he said. "There is a restaurant not too far away that delivers."

I knew the place he talked about. It was not cheap. I enjoyed Lai food a lot, but I rarely splurged on such luxuries.

"Don't worry," my neighbor said. "I'll pay."

Since the man had startled me into attacking him with a lamp, broken into my social media account, caused a horrible smell to linger in my living room, and made me wait for an hour, I decided he definitely owed me that much.

"Fine," I agreed and found the menu on my patch. I ran through the list, looking for my favorite spicy dish. "I'll have a 221b."

Raithan made an affirmative sound. "You know, I think I will too."

When the food arrived, it was delicious, but I could tell Raithan only had half of his attention on the meal. The rest of his mind was occupied with going through the case. I couldn't blame him. It was not my job, and even I was constantly mulling it over.

As I lay in my bed that night, it occurred to me that I had not had a moment of boredom since all this began. That I had, even despite the fatigue I suffered earlier in the day, felt better both mentally and physically, since Raithan WeinZalneinth appeared in my life. And I had no idea what to make of that.

CHAPTER IX
GREITHON SHOWS WHAT HE CAN DO

I woke up the next morning to a short dispatch from Raithan. *I have breakfast. Join me,* it said. My neighbor really was up frightfully early these days, but clearly he had no time for composing lengthy messages.

I dutifully got out of bed, went to the washroom to shower and arrange my hair. Then I dressed and went into our common room thinking that if Raithan could use that shortcut when he pleased, so could I. Raithan, however, was already in the common room and had breakfast laid out.

"You got me black brew?" I blurted because the singular smell was wafting at me.

Raithan smiled. He looked perfectly energized. His hair was braided near his scalp and then proceeded to fall in loose waves around his shoulders and down his back this morning. He was wearing a light purple shirt with a richly colored waist sash and pants a few tones darker than his hair. "Yes. And something called a crysant. Am I pronouncing it correctly?"

"Croissant," I said. I take pride in not maiming the few words I know in the languages of other species.

"Noted. Have a seat."

I did so and took a long, grateful mouthful of the black brew. It was distinctly better than the instant powder in my kitchen and I closed my eyes and savored the taste. "You are up early," I eventually said.

"Yes. Now that you know what I do, I don't mind explaining. It's how I work. When I'm on a case, I go all in."

"And out of your way to get breakfast," I noted.

"Only when I have a reason."

"You don't eat breakfast if you don't have a reason?" I asked. He was not underweight or even as naturally slender as I, but the bulk he had was clearly muscle.

"I do because I know my body needs fuel to work properly," he said, "but I'll happily drink a nutrient shake while I work."

"How very zetoi of you," I said.

"When it comes to efficiency, we have nothing on our galactic avian neighbors. Anyway," he changed the subject, "have you looked at the news yet?"

I had not. Because he had asked me for breakfast, and like a pet, I had answered the summons without question or delay. No, that wasn't fair. It was not obedience that drove me. It was interest in the case I was, apparently, assisting Raithan with, although my contribution wasn't very substantial.

"My Irregulars inform me that the various PlaNet news media are mentioning our case," Raithan said, and whether he noticed the plural pronoun or not, I have no idea. "And of course someone has leaked the most awkward things at this point. The Draspaarg writing on the wall, the problem with alien species on Ganmak, and a few reporters even try to paint the whole thing as something highly political that the government is trying to cover up. They speculate that perhaps Drebber was a victim of some kind of conspiracy. Lystrath and Greithon have both been interviewed, but thankfully they have not revealed anything they shouldn't."

"But the case is in the FWSA's hands now," I said through a mouthful of croissant. It was a light and fluffy kind of pastry native to a particular region on the human homeworld. "Why hasn't anyone talked to you?"

"Technically, I am working with the peace corps. Although I am in charge of the investigation, they are still part of it. And I prefer it this way. How often do you actually see interviews with a federal agent?"

Very rarely, I had to admit, if ever.

"We like to be discreet."

I had to stifle a snort of laughter at that. Raithan was one of the least discreet people I knew, and with his good looks, I doubted he went unnoticed anywhere.

"Ah," he said as if he read my mind, again, "but you forget one thing."

"And that is?" I asked.

"I control what people see and hear. The louder I am, visually speaking, the less people notice what I wish to keep to myself."

"Right," I said slowly. I wondered what he was keeping from me.

"Kellieth, I'm telling you this much, aren't I?" Raithan said, a note of slight irritation creeping into his voice.

"Yes. Why?" I asked.

I'm not sure he intended to answer, and in any case, he didn't get the chance because his patch lit up with an incoming call.

"And here is Greithon. Took him long enough," Raithan said under his breath and then, "No, do stay. I might want your input on this."

I had indeed been getting up to leave him to his call, but sat down again.

Raithan pulled up a display. It was angled so I could not see it, but Greithon's voice came through loud and clear.

"Good morning, agent," he said cheerfully.

"Good morning. You look like the syraxh who ate the warin today," Raithan replied.

"And with good reason!" Greithon said. "The whole thing is practically wrapped up. I hope you won't be too upset that I'm stealing your glory."

"I'm sure my glory is fine," Raithan said airily. "But if you are done gloating, perhaps you will share with me what has happened?"

"I caught the murderer."

There was a pause, and I saw Raithan's expression change ever so slightly before he got it back under control. "I see. Do go on."

"We managed to identify the dead human. His name is Enoch Drebber," said Greithon. He sounded pleased. "He came here from a human planet called Johnson along with a secretary called Johanna Stangerson on a business trip."

"Yes," Raithan agreed. "But the murderer, Greithon."

I was beginning to fathom that Raithan had still not shared any of the information he pulled from Drebber's patch with the peace corps.

Raithan caught my incredulous scent and looked over at me.

"You didn't tell them about the patch?" I mouthed.

If Raithan read my lips, he didn't make an indication of it.

"The murderer's name is Anne Charpentier," said Greithon. "A human, obviously. She's a former member of the Terran Defense Force. And we all know what that means."

Raithan relaxed into a smile. "Please enlighten me."

"Well, they are a brutal bunch, but not very smart," Greithon said. "Humans."

"Ah," Raithan replied, but his expression suggested he might as well have called Greithon a specieist to his face. "Care to tell me how you managed to catch this person, then?"

"Certainly. You know, Lystrath got this idea that Enoch's secretary is involved and is pursuing her. If you ask me, she could not be more wrong. Johanna might be useful to interview, but she is hardly the murderer."

"Hm," Raithan replied. "But your own line of pursuit, please?"

"Do you remember the scarf left at crime scene?"

"I do. It had the victim's name embroidered in one corner and was from a company called Bold and Bespoke," Raithan said.

"Well, it was from— What?" Greithon had clearly not expected Raithan to have picked up on that. I heard him draw in breath and could imagine how uncomfortable he looked so vividly that I had to stifle a laugh.

Raithan looked up at me again, but he kept his expression neutral.

"Have you followed up on the lead too?" Greithon demanded.

"No," Raithan said.

"Hah! Your lot could learn a thing or two from us hard-working peace corps. I got in touch with Bold and Bespoke and asked if they had a customer who matched Enoch's description. And they did, of course. They had custom-embroidered the scarf for him and delivered it, so I got the address of where he was staying at the time."

"Smart. Very smart," Raithan intoned.

"So I visited that address, of course," Greithon went on.

I will not be reproducing his story verbatim because it was embellished with quite a few self-glorifying asides and some ridicule of the humans involved that I find tasteless. But this is the gist of it:

Greithon had gone to the host house where Drebber and Stangerson stayed and found the human manager, Anne Charpentier. She was clearly distressed, and so was her daughter who was also present. This made Greithon think he was on the right scent. So he asked them if they had heard anything about Drebber, or Enoch as Greithon insisted on calling him as if it were a Menal name. They both confirmed that they had heard of the murder. Greithon questioned them on the spot and learned that Drebber and his traveling companion left in the evening the day before he was found dead. At first, the two humans denied seeing him again after that, but when Greithon told them he could smell they were hiding something, they broke down and confessed.

I am not saying that Drebber deserved what happened to him because that is not my place, and every person deserves the right to redeem themself. But the picture the pair of humans painted of Drebber was not pretty. He had lived in the host house for a three quarter month, claiming he was on a business journey. Stangerson was a quiet and polite person, but Drebber was unpleasant to say the least. He was lavish and indiscreet with his spending of units and tried to tip the staff, either not aware or not respecting what a social faux pas that is in this culture.

It is not uncommon for other species to misunderstand how host houses work, thinking that the company they offer guests is sexual in nature. In addition to this, certain species also look down on sex workers, and as a result, they can be quite offensive. I will admit that a host house operated by humans sounds a bit strange to me, but there is absolutely no reason it should not be able to work. But those speculations are neither here nor there.

Drebber was rude to most of the host house staff except a few girls, the owner's daughter included, whom he apparently tried to proposition several times. Allegedly, he said that one of his reasons for staying in a non-wendek establishment was to have access to alcohol. And this he enjoyed in great quantities, almost clearing out the entirety of the host house's stock of human spirits in the time he was there. The manager wanted to throw him out, but she was embarrassed to make a fuss and could use the units, too. But eventually she did turn Drebber and Stangerson out.

Nonetheless, Drebber did not stay away. A few hours later, he returned alone, saying he had had a fight with Stangerson and felt lonely. He was drunk and intent on Charpentier's daughter. He wanted her to come with him, to be his date for some party he was invited to. He even tried to physically drag her with him. It was at this point that the manager had enough and bodily forced him to leave. According to her, she only pulled Drebber outside and threatened him with calling the peace corps after a bit of a scuffle. And the next day, she and her daughter learned that Drebber was dead. No one could verify the story. There were no witnesses. But the manager was angry and told her daughter that she would go for a walk after getting rid of Drebber. She returned two hours later. Greithon's conclusion to this was that clearly, she had then taken Drebber to Salek Gardens and killed him there.

"Very interesting," Raithan interrupted at this point in the story. "What happened next?"

"Well, I took the manager with me on suspicion of murder, of course. I suspect you'll want to interview her," Greithon said.

I did not have Raithan's keen insight, but even I felt that something was off here. Was the host house manager supposed to walk around with lethal poison in a pocket? And besides, it was one thing to throw someone out of your establishment and another altogether to kill them. Even accounting for human temperaments, that was too extreme.

I wanted to tell Raithan to ask Greithon about the writing on the wall and the ring. Where would they fit into all this?

"I think you have gotten everything even remotely relevant out of that person," Raithan said. "So I will hold off questioning her myself, at least until I— Oh, I seem to have another incoming call. Do you mind if we add your colleague Lystrath to this conversation?"

"Not at all. I haven't told her about the murderer yet, and I'd like to see her face when she finds out I have it all figured out," Greithon said.

I was not oblivious to the fact that Raithan had let Greithon gloat although it was clear to me that he did not believe the peace corps had arrested the right person. I wondered if he'd do the same to Lystrath.

"Right," Raithan said, and a moment later, a second voice came from his display.

"Greithon. Raithan," said a subdued-sounding Lystrath. "I'll make this short. I was looking for the victim's secretary, Johanna Stangerson."

"Yes?" Raithan said, and I could tell from his tone that he was done playing.

"Did you find her? She didn't have anything to do with the murder, did she?" Greithon asked.

"Well, I found her all right," Lystrath said in a clipped sort of tone. "She was murdered in a self-service hotel a few hours ago."

Chapter X
LIGHT IN THE DARKNESS

Both Raithan and Greithon fell silent, and it was in that moment I discovered how utterly invested I had become in all this. I was never that into crime shows, and while I followed the news, it was not with the excitement at other people's misfortunes as some. But this was different. I had plunged into Raithan's world and been as immersed as an åayu in the sea.

Raithan's eyes narrowed. "Stangerson too," he said. "The plot thickens."

"It was quite thick enough before," said Lystrath. "But you two were already talking when I requested a connection. Anything I should know?"

"Are you absolutely sure?" Greithon asked. "Could she have... I don't know, had a heart attack? Humans get them too, right?"

"Yes, I'm sure!" Lystrath snapped. "I am literally standing five paces from her body. Does this look like a heart attack to you?"

"Well," Raithan said, studying an image I could not see from my vantage point, "something definitely attacked her heart. All right, Lystrath, let me have your location, and I will be there as soon as possible. Don't let anyone touch the body or tamper with the place."

"It's not exactly my first murder case," Lystrath grumbled.

"Here's the location."

"Thank you. I'll be with you shortly." Raithan did not waste any time saying goodbye to any of the peace corps investigators but collapsed the display right away. He stood up, went to his apartment without a word and returned to the common room in the process of putting on a harness with a gun holster. He fastened the straps and tugged once to make sure they were secure. Then he paused and looked at me as if he had completely forgotten I was there.

"Hi," I said, "I'm Kellieth ReinAraneinth. Remember me? I'm your neighbor, and I'm somehow involved in your double murder mystery."

"Yes," Raithan said slowly, breathing in my irritation. "Do you... want to come along?"

Had I assumed he wanted me to? And more importantly, did I really want to? Wasn't one dead human more than enough for me? I felt it really rather was. I had no desire at all to look at any murder victim, human, wendek or any other species. Yet, not insisting on coming along felt like backing down, and I did not get to this point in life by backing down from challenges. A small voice in the back of my head pointed out that "this point in life" was not exactly a glorious career, or a thriving social life, or very much of anything beyond a comfortable mug of black brew that was both bland and strong enough as not to remind me of my hyposmia. I straightened my back. I was not going to let self-pity dictate what I did or did not do. Mere moments before, I admitted to myself how invested I was. No, I found no joy in dead bodies, but I did find joy and meaning in scientific investigation, and this was the closest thing I would get right now.

"Yes," I said. "I'm a scientist. I am naturally curious. I want to see this through to the end."

Raithan sized me up with his steady, contemplative gaze. "This is a bit more... visceral than the previous murder," he said.

"Thank you for your concern, but I think I can handle it," I said with more bravado than I really felt.

"Then get your jacket," Raithan said, "and meet me outside."

A short while later, I was once again sitting next to Raithan in his groundwheeler. I noticed him disabling the automatic speed limitations on the vehicle and switch all controls to manual.

"Are we in a hurry?" I asked. He had not rushed to the first crime scene.

"Yes," Raithan said.

"Because..?" I prompted. "Are you afraid this victim will come back to life?"

"What?"

"I— that was what you joked about when you talked to Vanthein," I said, looking down at my interlaced fingers in my lap. Why was I feeling disrespectful when it was his joke in the first place?

"Oh, so I did," he said. It was not followed by his usual grin.

"So the actual reason we are in a hurry is..?" I tried again. "You are worried about something. What is it?"

"I want to catch the murderer. I'm afraid they might disappear now that they are done with what they came here to do."

"Which was killing the two humans?"

"Precisely. A smart person would leave Nantheam as soon as possible after that. Unless... Oh thak it, there's a traffic jam up ahead. Hang on." Raithan touched a panel on the hatch of the groundwheeler, and a siren began to wail. He swerved out of our lane and sped up. Of course he had a siren. Why was I even surprised?

Raithan's manual driving was efficient, and he only slowed down briefly to make way for pedestrians and sliders when needed. He brought us along the Ometha for a few minutes, and I sat looking out at the splendid waterfront of buildings gleaming in the morning light. We crossed one of the bridges to the other side and continued to a location in the Sein District.

Whether it was my neighbor's concentration on the traffic or his focus on the case he was investigating that caused it, he was silent until he stopped the groundwheeler near the location of the self-service hotel that Lystrath had specified. It was not an area I was particularly familiar with, though I had memories of going to a club not too far away with fellow students a few times. It was a traditional Menal venue serving vapors and not much else, and to my chagrin, I always ended up being the sober, responsible one who made sure everybody got home safely because I had, and have, to be careful with vapors. I prefer indulging in beverages when I do indulge. In any case, the area was the site of many such clubs, eateries and host houses and much busier in the evenings than at this time of the day.

The groundwheeler's hatch had closed behind Raithan before I even put my feet on the ground. I saw him study our surroundings, and by now, I could guess what sort of thing he was looking for. But he did not linger. Probably this street was far too busy and far too well-paved to be able to pick out any specific tire tracks or any other signs of the murderer.

The hotel ahead of us was a far cry from a host house. The words impersonal and universally palatable come to mind. Contrasted with its rowdy neighbors bearing colorful screens and brightly animated signs advertising what they offered, it stood there in sombre, muted brown hues, promising a no-nonsense approach to anyone who needed a place to sleep and nothing else.

When the door slid open to admit Raithan and me, we were greeted by an interior matching the exterior. Clean and in perfect repair, but with no luxuries and no friendly staff to help you plan your sightseeing or keep you company. Perhaps Stangerson had chosen it for the cheaper price tag, or to remain unnoticed.

Lystrath was waiting for us in the hotel's lobby. She was looking as neat and stern as ever. A transparent facemask was dangling on its strap around her neck, and this time I noticed she, like Raithan, was armed. Unlike him she wore her gun in a bulky holster at her hip and not concealed under a jacket.

"All right, take it from the top," Raithan said to her.

"And good day to you too, agent," Lystrath said under her breath. I sympathized with her. "Right, so according to Greithon, Enoch Drebber and Johanna Stangerson were both thrown out of their previous lodgings. Drebber was found dead only hours after that, and Stangerson was not seen again. I figured that she was somehow involved, and since she didn't contact the peace corps about her missing employer, it stood to reason to think that she had something to hide."

"One might think that," Raithan allowed.

"And she had to stay somewhere. So I checked every hotel and host house in Nantheam until I found the right one. This one. As you can tell, this isn't a staffed hotel."

Raithan made an affirmative gesture.

"But remote management could tell me a human checked in on the night when Enoch Drebber was murdered and that she hardly left her room since." An annoyed expression crossed Lystrath's face. "She used the name Stacy Johanson. Clearly a fake name. Well, management gave me the room number, so I decided to see what was going on with her."

"So you did that without consulting me first," Raithan observed.

"You're the leading investigator, not a babysitter," Lystrath said. "Well, I went up, and I didn't have to go far before I could smell her. Not the usual human odor. It was worse. Worse even than at the first crime scene. The door was locked, but I demanded that management open it for me because it was an emergency. And what I saw inside—"

"Yes, yes," Raithan said. "We don't need a dramatic retelling of that. Let's head up and see for ourselves."

"*He* doesn't need a dramatic retelling," Lystrath muttered as Raithan shouldered past her. "The man is a walking drama himself." She looked at me and made an apologetic gesture. "Sorry, I shouldn't..."

"No, no, it's fine," I reassured her. "I'm inclined to agree with you." Though every time I saw Raithan interact with her and Greithon, I could not help wondering about the past they shared.

Clearly, there was history between the three of them.

Johanna Stangerson's room was located on the 12th floor of the building. We rode the elevator up in silence, Lystrath standing with her hands clasped behind her back and feet a bit apart in a vaguely military way and Raithan leaning against the wall of the carriage with his eyes fixed on the display showing the floor numbers as if he could will it to go faster.

We exited and Lystrath led us a couple of doors down the empty, nondescript corridor to room B2. I thought I was prepared. I had known it would be bloody and attempted to steel myself for whatever was in that room. But I stopped in the door and had to steady myself on the frame.

The room was small and had only a bed and a closet for furnishing. A screen on the wall was looping advertisements aimed at tourists, which is the norm for self-service hotels. The window was open, and I was grateful for it. The smell was as horrid as Lystrath had indicated. Beside the window lay a huddled-up human figure. She was wearing what I assumed were her night clothes and looked very small and fragile with her exposed brown skin and undyed black hair. Blood was pooling under and around her.

"It's been a few hours," Raithan commented. He had slipped on a pair of forensic gloves and was examining the body, careful to not step in the blood.

"Yes," said Lystrath, squeezing past me into the room. "And the cause of death is plain for anyone with two nostrils." She was putting on her facemask. I regretted not bringing one and wondered how Raithan could stand it.

Raithan made a non-committal sound and bent closer to study the gaping wound in the human's chest. "The weapon did not hit the heart immediately, but it was twisted once inside and pierced it then. She bled to death," he said.

I reluctantly entered the room. Bleeding to death sounded like a slow way of dying. I hoped she would at least have been unconscious for some of that time.

"No murder weapon," Raithan concluded, "but it looks like a knife wound. Interesting..."

"Were you expecting poison?" I asked.

"Exactly, my dear Kellieth," Raithan said and stood up, facing me. "But it's clearly the same murderer." He pointed past me, and I felt panic creeping up on me as if he was gesturing at a villain standing right behind me. But then I turned and saw what he meant. The word *haenva* was scrawled in brownish letters on the light blue wall.

I moved closer and breathed in, trying to distinguish any smell from the stench in the rest of the room. But it was not so much the odor as the sight of the way the substance had coagulated that told me what it was. "This isn't black brew," I said.

"No, it's blood," Raithan agreed. "Human, I assume. Do you have anything on the killer, or should I see what my Irregulars can provide us with?" he continued to Lystrath.

"I was looking at surveillance when you arrived," she answered. "We have a clip of our perpetrator."

I moved over to Raithan to see the footage. It was a view of the hotel from the outside. It did not show the front entrance, but the back of the building which was not as exposed, I gathered.

A person approached it, and from their demeanor, you would not think it suspicious at all. There was no looking over their shoulder or hesitation. The person in the clip had a distinctly human look about them, and their hair was short and silvery. They set down a bucket on the ground, retrieved a drone from it, released it and, using a controller, sent it flying up and out of the camera's view. A few seconds later, a rope descended from the roof.

"Clever," noted Raithan. "They are disguised as a window cleaner."

"Really? I didn't think that was manual labor. Isn't it entirely left to robots or drones these days?" I asked as we watched the figure in the clip step into a harness at the end of the rope and be pulled up with the bucket in their hand.

"Usually," Lystrath said, "but you know how it is. Apparently there's a demand, so there are a few companies in Nantheam who advertise hands-on window cleaning. It's expensive, though, and not something you would expect a self-service hotel to have. I'm thinking we should check the cleaning companies and look for the killer among their employees."

"No," Raithan said. "There won't be any records. Notice the lack of company logos on the equipment and the person's clothes. These things were procured or made for the occasion."

The figure's ascent stopped at a window on the 12th floor, presumably the one in this very room. They worked with something we couldn't make out from the camera's angle, and then the window opened. They entered.

"After this, nothing happens until..." Lystrath sped up the recording, playing the next minutes in a few seconds. Then she slowed it down again. The figure crawled out of the window, let the harness take them back to the ground, retrieved the flying drone and bundled up everything in the bucket again. It was all impressively smooth. They never faced the camera directly as they left the scene, but I could tell they were around my height like Raithan had theorized.

Raithan tapped the display, skipped back a bit and froze and enlarged part of the image, studying the human's feet. The resolution was not great, but the automatic enhancement made it possible to discern part of the pattern on one sole. "That's our murderer, all right," Raithan said.

"Well, obviously. They were in this room and went to great lengths to use the window instead of a door," Lystrath argued.

"Yes, but there could be another reason for that. However, they match what I know about them. I don't suppose anything was stolen," Raithan said. He stepped across the body and opened the closet, examined what was inside, and then went back to the human. "She still has her patch," he said, indicating her wrist. And she is wearing jewelry. Kellieth?"

I stepped forward. "Yes?"

"Identify this for me."

I almost protested, but Raithan handed me a pair of forensic gloves, and then Stangerson's necklace caught my attention. So I put on the gloves, kneeled, very conscious of the blood on the floor, and carefully lifted the pendant from the dead human's collarbone. It was a warm shade of metal. "It's rose gold," I said.

"What's that?" Lystrath asked.

"It's an alloy. Pure gold mixed with a certain percentage of copper. Humans use it in jewelry a lot. It's especially popular because this particular alloy is not used very much, if at all, by other category 3 species. At one point, they got the idea that they might be able to copyright it, but..." I cleared my throat. "That is not important."

"Oh, but it is. Because a robber, especially a human robber, would recognize it as a potentially valuable metal and therefore take it," Raithan said.

"Yes," I agreed.

"All right, just one more thing left for me to do," Raithan said.

"You want me to take her patch and analyze it?" Lystrath asked. "Verify that it is her?"

"You can if you feel like it, but it's not going to make any difference to my investigation," Raithan said. "This, however, is." He leaned forward and then reached across the dead body to pick up something from under the bed. "The last link. My case is complete." He stood up, displaying a small cylindrical container with two capsules inside to Lystrath and me.

"Medication?" Lystrath asked.

"No, not unless you consider death a cure," Raithan said.

"Morbid," I muttered.

Lystrath made an exasperated noise.

"So, you think that's the poison?" I asked.

Raithan tapped the air. "Indeed. The killer left it here."

"But why? And why capsules?" Lystrath wondered.

"I am fairly certain they did not mean to stab Stangerson, but matters... escalated. As for why capsules, humans have a long history of using pills and capsules as recreational drugs as well as medication. Correct, Kellieth?"

"Yes," I agreed. "Despite the inefficiency, oral ingestion is still widely used in the human diaspora." I did not write any of my dissertations on humans, but I do have a rudimentary knowledge of these things.

"Now, to prove the theory," Raithan said. "Do you think we can find a pet somewhere that is close to dying anyway? Maybe we could visit a vet..."

"Hello?" I said, not without irritation at being overlooked for the second time in as many hours. "Chemist. I am literally right here. I can analyze those for you easily enough."

Raithan's grin told me he never intended to kill a pet and had really only wanted me to volunteer for the task. "Perfect. Lystrath, I will get back to you. Please try to keep from arresting anyone else, all right?"

"That was Greithon!" Lystrath protested. "You cannot hold me responsible for what that dimdek does to impress you!"

"Whatever," Raithan said. "Come on, Kellieth."

"Where are you going?" Lystrath called after us.

"To the Agency's labs," Raithan said.

I will admit I felt a jolt of excitement at the prospect.

"I have two questions," I said as we stood in the elevator again.

"Impressive," Raithan replied, "I find that most people have more."

I ignored this bit of cockiness. "You already know who the killer is. You have for a while. How?"

"It all comes down to deduction," Raithan said. "I have learned of their identity from the traces left at the crime scenes, from certain documents on Drebber's patch cryptically hinting at someone he and Stangerson wanted to avoid, and so on. Every step of the way, my initial theory has been corroborated."

"All right then," I continued. "But why do we need to analyze the pills, then? Why don't you just arrest them?"

"There are a few circumstances which make it impractical to attempt to apprehend them directly. And I want to lay out all the pieces when I hand over the case to the judicature. Especially since this concerns another species. It would be very nice, for instance, to be able to prove that this is a human-engineered poison and not a wendek one."

"That makes sense," I said.

"My plans usually do," Raithan commented.

CHAPTER XI

THE LAB, THE TRAP AND THE CHEMIST

The Federal Wendek Security Agency's headquarters are located in Weith District near the very center of our great city. It is a bustling district full of important institutions such as Ganmak's seat of government and foreign embassies. I have passed those backbones of our society often enough, especially when I was younger and commuted to the Institute of Science using public transport. Indeed, Raithan and I passed the Institute with its severe architectural symmetry on our way from the self-service hotel.

The FWSA building itself was a modern masterpiece according to those who had an expertise in architecture. I didn't, but I agreed; it took its point of departure in the style of the surrounding buildings, retaining the basic elegance of earlier times and adding to it a technologically advanced touch when it came to materials and over all appearance. It was, unlike its black and colorful neighbors, nearly entirely white. Even the many windows and transparent panels were tinted, which gave it an air of importance and severe secrecy that left onlookers slightly intimidated, myself included.

Raithan took us to a parking area where we left his groundwheeler. I almost had to run to keep up with his long strides as he approached the building, and I was too proud to ask him to slow down and too winded to ask him anything else.

A security guard stood at the broad front door. She was not uniformed per se, but her clothes suggested understated authority. She was wearing a white shirt, a nearly black jacket of a practical cut that allowed freedom of movement, and a pair of matching pants. A holster at her hip gave us a good view of the gun she was carrying, and she had a no-nonsense air about her. She was around Raithan's height and was heavyset in a way that suggested muscle.

Raithan greeted her and held up his identifier.

"Thank you. Welcome back, sir," the guard said. "What a surprise. First I don't smell you for more than a month, and now it's the second day in a row."

That was news to me. But then, I had been asleep for much of yesterday after we visited the first murder scene and Vanthein, and Raithan might very well have gone to the FWSA's headquarters during that time.

"I'm flattered you keep tabs on me," Raithan said.

"And you are?" the security guard continued to me.

"Chemistry Doyen Kellieth ReinAraneinth. I'm with him," I said, hoping that my title would make my visit here appear legitimate.

"They are. All of that," Raithan agreed.

The guard subtly moved to block our entrance. "There is a procedure for these things, agent. I need to see identification and—"

"We are in a bit of a hurry," Raithan said. "I need a chemist, I don't want to wait for one to have time for my request, and I promise on my honor as a defender of the wendek worlds that I am not smuggling a terrorist or a foreign agent into our stronghold. Kellieth, you are not a terrorist or a foreign agent, right?"

"No, I'm not," I replied, trying to smile politely and confidently at the guard.

"I am not saying you are," the guard told Raithan flatly. "And I realize you are a first class agent, but..."

"And I realize you have had a rough day what with the domestic issues you had this morning," Raithan snapped, "But that's not a reason to take it out on me."

The expression on the guard's face went through surprise and anger before settling on blankness. "I forgot you do that, Raithan WeinZalneinth," she said. "And I'll let you and your friend through if only because I don't want to listen to you while you rattle off what I had for lunch and when I last got a pair of shoes."

"Thank you," Raithan said. "A ripeth salad and yesterday afternoon," he added.

"Go away, agent," the guard said.

I made a vague apologetic gesture in her direction as we hurried into the building. "You were here yesterday and she was wearing a different pair of shoes, and these ones looked new?" I asked.

"My dear Doyen, you are catching on," Raithan exclaimed. "How very good. This way."

I was curious about his other deductions, but I sensed now was not the time. Raithan directed me to an elevator that, as it ascended, gave me a good look of the lobby area of the FWSA's headquarters. Like the building's exterior, the interior was frightfully white. It was daunting. Uniformed guards at every corner, people taking calls and offering assistance to visitors. It was clearly a busy hub, but the offices with agents drinking stimulating twa and pouring over secret documents or interrogating reluctant criminals that entertainment had led me to expect were nowhere to be seen. Probably, these things took place in less public spaces, which made perfect sense.

The elevator stopped, and we stepped into a rather bland, yellow-painted corridor. I could not help but wonder if all the white downstairs was for the sake of the public who never got to see other parts of the premises.

Raithan took me through several of these anonymous corridors, past rooms with tastefully toned glass panes and doors behind which I glimpsed offices. Some of them were occupied, others not. And some of the transparent walls were obscured by shutters.

"Here we are," Raithan finally said, scanning his identifier at a door. The shutters were down, so it was only when the door slid open that I saw the nature of the room. And what a nature. Embarrassing as it is to admit, it nearly made me whimper with longing.

It was the state-of-the-art lab of any unemployed chemist's dreams. Clean, metallic surfaces, cupboards containing beakers and sample dishes. Analyzing equipment of every kind, from classic centrifuges to the latest models of subatomic scanners, which I have read about but never even had the chance to touch.

"Do you need a moment?" Raithan whispered in my ear.

"I— No, I'm fine. It's just beautiful," I said, knowing how embarrassed I probably smelled.

"Does it have what you need for analyzing the capsules?"

"Yes. It has everything."

"Good. I brought this too. I am already convinced, but we might as well verify that it is the same poison used on both victims." Raithan handed me the sealed bag with the disposable cup from the first crime scene.

"Of course," I said. "That is simple enough."

"Then get to work."

I did not even balk or protest at Raithan's ordering me around. Standing there, I felt the gravity of how badly I missed my work. I put the bag with the cup on the workbench, sat down on the kind of stool that is endemic to every lab I have worked in and pulled a standard analysis array closer. Raithan placed the capsules in the glass in front of me.

"You don't need to destroy them, right?" he asked. "I should prefer to keep them as evidence."

I chuckled. "This is cutting edge technology, Raithan. You will hardly be able to tell I have been tampering with them."

"Good. Is there anything else you need?"

I looked up at him. He was feeling useless now. Things were out of his control. Two feelings he most decidedly did not like. "How about lunch?" I asked. "There must be food somewhere in this fancy building."

"Are you hungry?"

"A little, but I'm mostly thinking about you. Our breakfast was cut short, remember?" I said, making my way to the cabinet where the security equipment would be stored. It was not fear that anything may blow up in my face that drove me. It is simply second nature to any lab technician and chemist to eliminate contamination of any kind regardless of the work they set out to do.

I noticed Raithan eying me in a very particular way.

"I am not thin and easily exhausted because I don't eat," I told him. "I am thin and easily exhausted because I was ill. And besides, a person's body shape has nothing to do with whether it is in need of sustenance. Now, go away and get us lunch."

"All right. I will demonstrate to you the culinary expertise of the Agency's catering service," Raithan said and disappeared.

The wonderful lab provided me with a facemask and gloves, the former of which was as state-of-the art as everything else here. It only obstructed my breathing a little bit. I pulled down the containment case and began my work.

First, I took the cup out of the evidence bag. The black brew inside it was still moist, like Raithan had promised, and I extracted a few drops. Then I ran the subject matter through a number of different analyses in order to identify the poison. It turned out my first guess was accurate. In addition to black brew, the substance included a compound hathnitrate.

I did not think there was any real reason to determine where the black brew was made, but my enthusiasm at having this place at my disposal had me run an analysis of the components nevertheless. Finding the one that stood out from the generic ingredients present in any black brew was not hard, and accessing one of the huge PlaNet databases I had frequented in my student life to search for its origin was even easier.

My next action was to pick up one of the capsules. It was oblong and a silvery hue that gleamed in the light of the lamp I pulled close for a preliminary ocular examination. There was a protective outer film and a thin line around the middle where the capsule was put together. I found the smallest drill the lab had to offer for manual use, made a tiny hole through the outer film and collected a little bit of the fine granulate inside for a similar analysis. I was expecting compound hathnitrate again, but what I got was a completely harmless composition. It consisted mostly of a kind of starch, common, my cursory research told me, in human food. It was not even remotely poisonous to me, and evidently it was not to humans either.

I swiped away the display hovering above the table and considered the situation. Was Raithan wrong? Was I wrong? Were these capsules completely irrelevant to the case? No. I refused to believe that. If they were indeed Johanna Stangerson's own medication, they would contain a lot more than starch. But there was nothing difficult about the analyses I had performed. So why— I blinked. Oh.

I repeated the whole process on the other capsule. It had a hint of the same type of starch, but apart from that, it was saturated with, indeed, the same potent hathnitrate as the black brew. The substance was often present in fertilizer used by human planetformers, but the concentration in this capsule was alarmingly high. If it was proportionally applied to a fertilizer, it would not make anything grow. It would kill the crops and contaminate the soil severely. In the case of the capsule, it was, pardon the pun, overkill. Less than half a capsule would be lethal to me, and it no doubt would to a human as well.

I was feeling remarkably well by the time Raithan returned to the lab. Analyzing two apparently identical capsules was not exactly groundbreaking work, but it was wonderful to be back in a lab, and it felt nice to be helping Raithan's investigation.

"You have finished, I see," my federal agent neighbor remarked. He was carrying a tray with a couple of water bottles and two vegetable rolls which he began to set down on the work table.

"Not there!" I exclaimed, standing up to, if necessary, throw myself bodily across the room to keep foodstuffs away from anything sensitive. No, I had not left poisonous dust on the table, but no one wants darnell leaves in their microscope or sweet oil dressing sticking to their work surface.

"Then where?" he asked, a little exasperated, which I could understand. It was I who had told him to get us lunch, after all.

"Over there for now," I said, gesturing to an unused table by the door. "We can eat once I've told you what I found."

He obeyed and returned to me. "So, what is your verdict, Doyen?"

"The black brew was almost certainly imported from the human planet Hawking," I told him. "I don't believe it's particularly relevant, but..."

"But you said you could find out, and therefore you did," Raithan finished for me, clearly amused.

"Exactly." I smiled, and then sobered up as I pointed at the glass into which I had returned one of the capsules. "I analyzed that," I said, "and it is completely harmless to wendek and humans."

A shadow of doubt crossed Raithan's face. "Ah," he then said. "And the other one?"

Trust him to immediately see the conclusion to what would have been my little performance. "Yes," I said, "it has a large concentration of poison. Compound hathnitrate as I suspected. As for the disposable cup, there are traces of the same poison in the black brew."

"Which I assume corresponds with Mr. Drebber's symptoms?" Raithan asked.

"Indeed."

"Excellent work," Raithan said. "And you were right about the capsules too. I can't tell you tampered with them at all."

I felt simultaneously pleased by his acknowledgment of my work and annoyed because a simple analysis and a VoidSearch hardly demonstrated my skills.

"Now that you know the exact components," Raithan continued, "Can you make an antidote?"

I stared at him. "I don't have to." Really? He was one of those people who thought I would reverse-engineer the poison to create a specific antidote that worked on that one poison? I have noted before that I am certain Raithan likes to explain his deductions and impress his audience. In all honesty, I suffer from the same scholarly vice, though to a lesser degree.

I removed my inhaler from my pocket and showed it to him. "You identified this as the solution when you saw me struggling the first time we met. My particular respiratory dysfunction is caused by something specific, something rare. And my asthmatic episodes are triggered by factors that are not the same for everyone suffering from similar conditions. But the treatment is the same. If the problem was, say, choking on a foreign object, the treatment would be different."

"That was a lot of words to make your point, simple as it is," Raithan said. "One antidote is not needed for a specific poison, but you have to identify the type of poison to pick the right one, yes?"

"Exactly," I said, pointing at him with my inhaler. "So I am looking at how the poison enters the body and what type of poison it is and then I identify which type of antidote is the most helpful and how to administer it. But I will stress that it is not a miraculous cure. Swallowing that capsule would still cause a lot of unpleasantness even if the antidote was administered directly. It would just not be lethal. But," I added, seeing his amused expression and starting to feel somewhat embarrassed, "you already know that."

"Yes," he said. "And were you able to confirm that it is made by a human?"

"I can tell you that the outer layer of the capsules contain starch used in human foodstuffs and that the harmful component in the one that has it is common in human agricultural fertilizers and that no other species uses that exact compound."

"Good enough for me," Raithan said. "Now, do you want your lunch or not?"

*

The vegetable rolls were delicious. Not the standard all-needs-covered-at-an-affordable-price food I was used to from anywhere I had ever worked, but actually delicious. They also smelled wonderful even to me. "So," I asked after chasing down a bite with a mouthful of cold water, "what now?"

"Now we have all we need to catch the killer," Raithan said.

"We do?"

"I confirmed a few things while you were working." He was scrutinizing me now. "The question is whether you will help. How do you feel?"

"I have gone along with you so far, haven't I?" My tone was light, but the truth was that I felt better than I had ever since I got back to Ganmak. Even a short while in a lab doing actual work felt so good. Helping Raithan felt good.

"But how do you feel physically?" he insisted.

"I feel..." I took a deep breath. The climate control in the building was immaculate, and I could just pick up on a pleasant scent from a nearby censer. My breathing was unhindered, and I was hydrated and fed. "I feel fine. What do you need me to do?"

"I need you to trust me."

I scoffed at that line. "Really? That's all?"

"That's all," Raithan said with a smile that would not have looked out of place on a draever's face. "Drink up and come with me."

A short while later, I found myself in what I imagined a theater's dressing room would look like.

"You, my dear Kellieth," Raithan said and steered me toward a stool in front of a mirror, "are going undercover for a bit."

"What? But I'm not an agent like you," I protested.

"Nor do you have to be. I will do the agenting. You just need to drink a cup of black brew and go for a trip in a rent ride."

I met his eyes in the mirror. His expression was sincere. But... "If that is all," I said, "then why are we here? Why do I feel like you are about to cut my hair?"

"I wouldn't dream of it," Raithan said. "But I am going to give you a temporary makeover. I am, you see, very good at disguises,"

"And you want to disguise me and not yourself? Why?"

"Because in this case I would never be able to play the part. But you will."

"And what is that part?"

"Someone who will be inconspicuous to our target. Now, sit still and let me work." Raithan stepped in between me and the mirror, effectively keeping me from seeing what he was doing. From the feeling of it, I guessed he was removing my sparse amount of makeup and applying something a lot more substantial with a smell I couldn't quite place. Now and then, he would step back and assess his work and then continue. When he was finally happy with it, he stood aside and let me see.

I was beige. My normal skin color was completely covered, and it looked unsettling. But I had to admit Raithan had done a good job of making it look natural, or as natural as that color could look, with shading and highlights and even some imperfections. "Am I supposed to look human?" I asked.

"Yes. Now, excuse me for a moment."

In the mirror, I watched him leave through a side door in the room. I sat looking as awkward as I felt, and it occurred to me that probably a human would feel as weird about having their skin painted grey as I did about this.

Raithan quickly returned with a handful of garments. "Here. Put these on," he said.

They were human, of course. I went along with it, stripped out of my own clothes and into a strange ensemble including a pair of light, skin-colored - that is wendek skin - pants and a huge, ill-fitting shirt with a hood. Finally, Raithan arranged a floppy oversized sock of a hat on my head to hide my ears. Then he adjusted the fabric of the shirt, fumbling a bit with the pocket on the front.

I stared at my reflection. It was uncanny.

"As I thought," Raithan said. "You make a convincing human."

"Thanks a lot," I said with poorly hidden sarcasm.

"A remarkably attractive human," Raithan amended.

I couldn't help laughing.

"I am going to drop you off at Diogenes where you will spend a bit of time before hiring a rent ride and doing exactly what I say."

"And what will you be doing? While I, presumably, go under cover as a human to somehow help catch the suspect?"

"I will be making preparations for the finale," he said, which was all I was getting out of him. "Come on. Time for a test run."

We went back to the ground floor, through the lobby and outside.

"Good day," Raithan said to the security guard.

"Good day, agent..." She trailed off. "Halt! Raithan, who is that?"

Raithan and I turned to her. "What do you mean?" Raithan asked innocently.

"Who is this? Why was there a human in HQ? Where is that chemist you brought in earlier?"

"Take a deep breath," Raithan advised. "I'm sure you weren't hired for your eyesight alone."

She looked annoyed but did what Raithan asked. Her eyes went round. "But how? It *is* them!"

Raithan bowed to her. "Thank you. See?" he continued to me, "You do make a believable human."

"The prettiest human I ever saw, though," the guard said.

"Thank you," I told her. In truth, humans are not necessarily ugly. You only have to look beyond the aesthetics you're used to.

"Let's go over the plan," Raithan said once we were back in his groundwheeler. I understood two things when he explained it. One; it really was as simple as he had advertised. And two; it was a plan that relied very much on my acting skills and, quite frankly, willingness to be bait.

"Not bait. More of a facilitator," Raithan corrected me.

"You are using me to get to the target. That is a bait," I argued.

"If you insist."

"I should have brought my shocker," I mused. "You don't happen to have one I can borrow, do you?"

"No," Raithan said, "on both accounts. Your being armed would paint a rather different picture of you than what we want. So... Do you need to go over the plan again?"

"No," I said.

"Are you sure? I sometimes forget how other people's minds work," Raithan said. "And it is extremely important that you do everything exactly as I have told you."

"Yes, I am sure," I said. "I'm sure my plain and ordinary mind is no match for your brilliance, but I can follow simple instructions."

CHAPTER XII
THE RENT RIDE

Once again, I found myself outside Diogenes where, in a manner of speaking, all this began. I watched Raithan's groundwheeler speed away and, not for the first time, wondered what I had gotten myself into. I was fully aware that curiosity regarding my new neighbor was not a sufficient explanation for why I was now so involved with Raithan's plan to catch a murderer that I was standing in the street disguised as a beige alien. Was I doing this out of gratitude for his letting me work in a lab once again? No. Although I was grateful for that, there was more to this.

I caught a glimpse of my reflection in the eatery's window and promptly changed my posture. Our physiques are very similar, but a human slouch looks very different from a wendek slouch. Probably it has something to do with the natural curve of their spine.

When I entered, a few people glanced up from their food and beverages. Two of them were wendek and one was human, and only one of the wendek appeared puzzled. Still, he quickly dismissed whatever had made him wonder about my appearance. Probably, it was my smell, or more accurately the lack of the usual human odors.

I ordered a cup of black brew and sat down at an empty table to drink it and while away some time before the real challenge began.

At this point, one of the patrons, who had not previously seemed to notice me, looked up from her patch and smiled. Her table was close to mine; this eatery adhered more to human standards than wendek, so the scents of different meals were free to mix.

"Hello," she said in Standard.

"Hi," I said, trying to look like I was not anticipating being asked why I was pretending to be human at any moment.

"Do you live here?" she asked.

"Yes, I'm studying chemistry at the Institute of Science," I said. Lies are easier to maintain if they are close to the truth. My skin is naturally smoother than that of most adult humans, and while Raithan had applied the facepaint expertly, he had not been able to or had not thought to fake folds and creases. And my build would suggest youth in a human as well, so passing for a student seemed quite possible.

"That's exciting. It is one of the best schools in the galaxy," the woman said. She was right. The Nantheam Institute of Science was prestigious because it had such high standards. I could have studied chemistry on my homeworld, Tewamak, but I had applied for Nantheam despite chances being slim. Evidently, my credentials and grades had paved the way for me.

"I'm happy I got in," I said, smiling and remembering to show my teeth.

The woman looked slightly taken aback, and I wondered if I was overdoing it. "Anyway, I like your tea," she said.

"My tea?" I repeated.

She pointed at her own cup. "The human drink tea. That's what I am having. This is called mint tea, but it tastes nothing like mynth."

"Oh. I see," I said. Was I supposed to thank her for the compliment on the behalf of humankind?

"So, how are you liking Nantheam?" she asked.

The question took me aback a little because spending a lot of time in a place naturally dulls your senses to its uniqueness. But Nantheam was different from any other city I had ever lived in or visited. It was steeped in millennia of culture and history and had grown organically rather than being meticulously planned and established mere centuries ago. I am sure other places on Ganmak have a similar history, but with Nantheam being the biggest metropolis and holding a central political position, it stood out. This is going to sound profoundly unscientific, and I apologize for that, but if you know Nantheam, you will know what I mean when I say the weather and climate here feel more like moods and whims of the city than natural phenomena. Nantheam feels alive, like a vast and complex entity. As if the lives our Creators gave Ganmak in order for it to thrive in mythical tales seeped into the foundations of the city as well. However, I digress. "It is such a vibrant city," I said out loud. "I like it here."

"I'm glad to hear that." The woman took a mouthful of her tea. "I hope you are feeling welcome. I know we can be a little intimidating."

"Oh, I am," I reassured her. "My... roommate is very different from me, but we get along well."

"That's good. Anyway, I really just wanted to compliment you," she continued. "You're different from most humans I've met." Her nostrils flared briefly. I didn't smell very much was what she meant.

"Thank you," I said, uncomfortably.

At that point, she received a message on her patch that she turned her attention to, and I was grateful for it. I'm no stranger to casual ableism, but there was something unsettling about the vague kind of speciesism I had just been subjected to. It was made no better by the fact that my fellow wendek had said nothing I didn't personally feel about humans as well.

Shortly after, I filed the episode for later consideration because it was time to act. I found the contact info of the rent ride company that Raithan had told me to use and made a call, insisting on talking to a staff member and not an automated system.

"Hi," I said in Standard when I got through after a few minutes. "My name is Kelly Reinhardt." I gave the operator the address of the eatery and then added, a little embarrassed, "Um, I was wondering if that nice human driver is available?"

"Which one?" asked the operator whose Standard had a clear Menal accent. I hoped I was disguising my own well enough.

"I can't remember the name, but I can give you a description," I said and proceeded to tell the operator what Raithan had instructed me to, from the approximate height and build to the hair color and length. "It was so nice not to have to... Well, worry about smells."

"Right," the operator said. "We have a few drivers of other species. A couple of draevere too."

"But I would really like the same one," I insisted. "Can you check if one of your drivers matches the description? I will give you a full score on WinWen and even write a review."

There was a pause. "All right," said the operator finally, sucked in by my promise or desperation. "I know the one you're talking about. He isn't free right now, but he should be soon."

"I don't mind waiting for him," I said, hoping all this wasn't too suspicious. "We just... hit it off really well."

"All right. I'll book you a ride with him. You'll get a message on your patch when he's in your area."

"Thank you so, so much," I said with genuine relief. "Um, but please don't tell him I asked for him. I don't want to seem like a creep. I'm honestly not a creep."

"Sure," the operator said. "Don't forget those seven protheran stars on WinWen."

I wrote the operator a glowing review and ordered another cup of black brew. Then I sent a dispatch to Raithan informing him of the situation.

"Very well," he responded. "Let me know when you get the update from the rent ride company and do not contact me again after that. Remember to stick to the plan no matter what."

Did he think I would seat myself next to the driver and hold up my patch so he could clearly see what I was telling my federal agent neighbor?

A little while later, I received a message that my rent ride would arrive shortly and notified Raithan. Then I left Diogenes and stood by the side of the street. Within a few moments, a rent ride slid to a halt next to me. I took a deep breath that was unrelated to my respiratory system and very related to the prospect of what I was about to do.

The back hatch opened. "Are you Kelly Reinhardt?" asked the human driver in Standard. He was around my height and lot broader around the shoulders, and I was glad I was wearing layers of baggy clothes because otherwise I would probably have looked like a horribly malnourished human child to him when in reality I was only a short and skinny wendek. His skin was a darker and more pink shade of beige than mine, and his features were rough and with badly shaved facial hair.

"Yes, I am," I said. I slid into the backseat and succeeded in not flinching when the hatch closed and left me alone in a rent ride with a murderer.

The man who killed Enoch Drebber and Johanna Stangerson said something that made absolutely no sense. He was speaking a human language at me. Of course. Like I spoke Menal or Synal to most of the people I knew. "Pardon," I said. "I don't speak... English." I hoped I was right that it was English. It was the only human language I could remember the name of and I was pretty sure it was widespread.

"What do you speak then?" he asked in Standard, turning around to study me over the back of his seat. His eyes were an astonishing blue color. "German? Your name sounds German."

"Yes, that's right," I said, relieved that he was handing me this one. "I am originally from a German settlement." I hoped German settlements existed.

"I see. Where do you need to get to?" he asked.

I gave him the address that Raithan had given me.

"All right," the driver said and slid back into the traffic. "We should be there in a half hour."

"That's great," I said, resisting the urge to fidget with anything.

"You asked for me to drive you?" he said.

My smile froze. Oh no. The operator had told him. "Yes, that's right," I said as offhandedly as I could muster. "I have had some bad experiences with wendek drivers. I mean, I don't want to sound touchy, but they can be a bit... speciesist."

"Tell me about it." His voice was low and raspy and had an interesting resonance, a deep sort of rumble. It was hard to tell how old he was. His hair was undyed and a silvery grey color, which might, unlike the natural hair of Hussa and many other Lai people, be an indication of age. He also had creases and lines on his face, but humans age faster and more radically than wendek. "They all think they're so high and mighty. Superior to everyone else in the galaxy when they are just a bunch of teched-up elves."

"Right, teched-up elves," I echoed and went for another teeth-baring smile. I had no idea what that meant, but decided to look it up later. Under different circumstances, experiencing humans and their view on us from an inside perspective would be an interesting learning situation. Studies could be made like this, if I were a different kind of scholar.

"But you didn't just ask for a human driver," he said. "You asked for me *specifically*."

I cleared my throat. I had to follow my nose on this one because Raithan was not here to instruct me. How had he not anticipated this scenario? Why had we relied on the operator to do what I asked? "Yes, because you drove me once before," I said without missing too many beats.

"No, I didn't," he said.

"Yes," I insisted because there was no backing down now. "It was a while ago, and I was wearing tinted glasses." And the man could not possibly remember every person he took for a ride when he did this for a living.

"No," he persisted. "I have a very good memory for faces and people. I have never given you a ride before."

I resisted the impulse to throw my head back and instead shook it from side to side like humans do to show denial. "I think the operator got it wrong, actually. I mean, you look like the person who drove me, but maybe you aren't. Is there another hu— person of your description in the rent ride company?"

"No," the driver said.

"Huh." I laughed weakly. "I wonder if I'm misremembering, then. It could be a different company altogether. In any case, I'm very sorry for the misunderstanding."

The human murderer turned to look at me again. He was not convinced. Not at all. And how had we ever expected this to work? How had Raithan of all people expected this to work? I consistently perform well in intelligence tests, and I considered him to be far above my level. So how... I blinked. Had we both underestimated this man because he was human? Was that it?

"I think you had better tell me the truth," the driver said.

"What are you talking about?" I asked with another weak chuckle. "I misremembered. Or you did. That's all."

The groundwheeler slowed down and stopped. We had reached an intersection, and I reached a decision. It was reckless of Raithan to set me on this task. I was not a trained agent. I was just a chemist with hyposmia and respiratory issues trying to get back on their feet after being very ill, that was all. I was playing along with my neighbor because he was charming and interesting and because I was desperate to do something with my life, but this... This was as far as I would go.

I moved quickly, throwing myself across the seat with the intention of hitting the panel that opened the passenger hatch so I could escape the rent ride. The killer might follow me, but hopefully I would be able to seek sanctuary in one of the shops nearby and call Raithan to tell him what had happened.

Just before I slammed my hand down on the panel, it emitted a soft click. And it did not react to my touch.

"Oh no, you don't," the driver told me.

I straightened up and looked at him, but he was intent on the road ahead now. The rent ride started moving again. "Now, why don't you tell me the truth?" he asked.

I swallowed. And laughed, which was half a hysterical response to the whole situation and half an attempt to fool him. If I could come up with a good enough story, he just might believe me. "All right, you have me," I said and pulled off my sock hat to reveal my ears. "I'm actually not human. I'm wendek."

"Your disguise is good," he said conversationally.

"Thank you," I replied, generating a cover story even as I spoke. "I am working on an article about speciesism, and I wanted a human driver so I could ask them how it is to work as an alien on a wendek world. But I didn't want anyone to get defensive, so I thought disguising myself was the best way."

"Nice try," my driver said. "No one would go to such lengths when you could hire a human to do the interview for you. You are working for the peace corps."

"What? No!" I protested. "You have it all wrong! What would a peace corps officer even want with a human rent ride driver?" I had to do something. The hatch was locked. I had botched my attempt at a plausible story. If only I had brought a shocker after all, I might be able to threaten him to stop and let me out. Very slowly, I brought my fingers to my wrist. If I could call Raithan and let him hear what was going on...

"Don't even think about it," my driver told me.

I swallowed and glanced out of the window. Raithan had to be tracking my patch anyway, right? "Where are you taking me?" Because, I realized, he was definitely not going to the location where Raithan was waiting for us. I had been too preoccupied with trying to seem inconspicuous, and failing, to discover this earlier.

"We're just going for a little ride, you and me," he said.

We were still in the city. There were people in the streets. I could get somebody's attention. Alert someone, anyone, to the fact that I was getting abducted. I threw myself against the window and began to strike at it with my fists, shouting for help as loudly as I could.

"Stop that!" my driver bellowed.

I didn't.

"I said, stop it!" he told me again with such vehemence that my eyes were drawn to him. He was steering the groundwheeler with one hand and had twisted so he was pointing something at me. A gun? No, not a gun. It was a small spray bottle. He pressed down the button on top of it, and a misty vapor rushed out. I instinctively stopped breathing. What was that? Poison? But then he would be poisoned too. It had to be something that would not affect humans because he was not wearing protection, and he had to be able to keep driving.

"Stop fighting, wendek," he told me.

And eventually my body betrayed me and took a deep gulp of air. I spend so much time trying to breathe normally, pretending to be affected by smells and pheromones in the same way that everyone around me is. But in truth, only my sense of smell is deficient. What reaches my lungs affects me in exactly the same way it would other people. And for once, I wished it wasn't so. The air that rushed into my mouth made me gag and cough. It was not legal to possess this kind of spray, but this human was a murderer and probably did not care about such details. I fumbled for my inhaler because maybe, just maybe, the emergency medication in it could counteract whatever this was, but I dropped it on the floor. My movements were so clumsy. My vision was growing dim. There was something wet on my face. My nose was bleeding, I discovered when I tasted it. I fought to breathe, to throw myself against the window again to get somebody's attention, but somehow I missed and wound up smashing the side of my face into the hatch. It should probably hurt. It didn't. And that was my last thought before the vapor took its full effect.

Chapter XIII
IN THE VERDANT

The world around me was shaking, and as a result, my teeth chattered, and the side of my head rattled against something hard. I had no idea where I was or what had happened. Only that something was dangerously amiss and that it was merely peripherally connected to the shaking world. I fought my way out of the darkness and forced my eyes open. I was half sitting, slumped against a vibrating wall. My mouth tasted like blood, and my nose felt blocked. Had I had a bad asthmatic episode? No, this was something else. I blinked a few times. I was in a groundwheeler... And that was the moment everything came back. I lurched to an upright position and immediately regretted the sudden movement.

"Are you going to behave now?" the driver of the groundwheeler demanded. The human. The murderer.

"Where are we going?" I asked thickly. Judging from the greenery outside the window, we were not in the city anymore. And if the rattling of the rent ride was anything to go by, we had gone off road altogether. I surmised that we were in the Verdant, the nature reservation cradling Nantheam on its south and west sides. For how long had I been insensible?

"For a ride. This is a rent ride, after all," the murderer said.

"I should very much like to go to my original destination, then." My voice was still a little wobbly, but I had regained my faculties, even if my head pounded, and every jolt of the groundwheeler made it worse. I glanced at my wrist to determine how much time had passed, but my patch was gone. That was bad. I had assumed Raithan and his Irregulars could use its signal to track me in case of an emergency.

"I don't think so."

"Can I do anything to convince you?" I asked. "There must be something you want. Money? Freedom?"

"I want freedom," he mused.

"Then—"

"I want freedom," he repeated, more loudly. "I want to be free from this burden I have been carrying for years."

"Maybe I can help," I told him as earnestly as I possibly could given the circumstances. "What kind of burden? Do you want to talk about it?"

The driver barked out a short laugh. "You were never in my plan, you know," he said.

"It's not too late to let me out," I returned. "You can stop right here, let me out and leave, and you will never hear from me again." Because yes, he was a murderer who deserved to be brought to justice, but I was powerless in this situation, and I could not see how sacrificing myself would make any difference at all.

"Did you not ask me to share my burden with you?" he asked.

"That's an option too. How about you tell me about it, and then we will see if maybe I can give you some advice?" If I could stall him for long enough, perhaps Raithan would be able to find me. I might not have my patch anymore, but maybe he could... I imagined him somehow being able to follow the rent ride, smelling its route or... No. Formidable as his abilities were, even Raithan could not do that. But maybe his Irregulars could locate the groundwheeler. Surely, he must at least have taken some kind of action when I failed to show up at the agreed upon location. For now, however, I was on my own.

My driver stopped the groundwheeler. What now? He opened the front hatch and went around the vehicle to open the back hatch too. "Come on," he said and grabbed my arm with fingers that almost closed all the way around my bicep. He dragged me out, and my feet found the soft ground as I stumbled into the warm light of the late afternoon.

Centuries ago, the area south and west of Nantheam was turned into a nature reservation when our species began to take seriously the negative footprints we were leaving on Ganmak by exploiting our homeworld's resources. I once watched a time lapse clip of it where you can see how it went from mining areas and farmland with a few copses of trees to a sprawling, green haven with wild animals and trunks so tall they almost match the tallest building in their neighboring city.

We were now standing somewhere in that haven on a footpath overgrown with lush, blue-green grass and delicate pink flowers. I felt strangely sad that I did not know their name.

"Wait," I said, "my inhaler." I had dropped it in the rent ride, and it must still be on the floor somewhere.

"You might not need to breathe for long," the murderer said.

Cold dread spiraled all the way up from my feet and into my chest. I tried to jerk away from him, but he pulled me closer without much effort. His hands were meaty and pink and had hairs on them. "Please," I tried, "I have no idea what's going on. I am no threat to you. There's no reason to kill me."

"I'm not going to kill you," he said.

He wasn't? His previous words had sounded very much like a threat to me.

"We're just going to talk, and then we'll play a little game."

A game. Under different circumstances that could have been an innocent proposal, but he was a murderer who had abducted me. I was not keen on playing anything with him. But, I reminded myself, the more time we spent on him not killing me, the better. "What kind of game?" I asked.

We were already deep in the Verdant, and every brisk step took us further in. The human was still holding my arm tightly and squeezing harder every time I slowed down or lost my footing on the uneven ground.

My breathing was labored, but thankfully not turning into an asthma attack despite the exertion, the vapor and the humid air. The nauseating headache was gradually subsiding, probably the upside of said air.

My abductor took me on a scenic route that I was in no position to appreciate at the time. The leaves on the trees around us were a light yellow with green spots and three times the size of my hands. The canopies nearly touched above our heads and dappled the ground with dancing shadows, and a breeze wafted the scents of flowers and foliage at us. As the path curved, a small lake peeked out from the vegetation, the water glittering invitingly at us. Probably, it was an old mine that had been converted into a lake. The kind you are warned about in your childhood because they look serene on the surface but can be practically bottomless pits of icy water.

"Sit," he finally told me, indicating a tree trunk that lay in the grass. Its bark was rough and overgrown with moss in places.

I sat. He didn't.

"I am going to tell you a story," he said. "Can you write, wendek?"

"Yes," I replied, trying to breathe deeply and get myself under control. Couldn't he?

He reached into a pocket, and I involuntarily flinched. But what he withdrew was not a gun or a spray can. It was a folded up bundle of papers and a cheap calligraphy pen, the kind with an inbuilt ink reservoir, which he thrust at me.

"You want me to write on paper?" I asked.

"You lost your patch, didn't you?"

I tried not to glare. He had clearly taken it off my wrist while I was unconscious and thrown it away or destroyed it.

"Only one of us is leaving this place alive," the human said, "If it is you, I want you to carry my story with you. If it is me, I will leave the papers on your body for others to discover after I am gone."

A confession, then. I had a fair idea of the game he was going to play now, and I fervently wished I had picked up an antidote for the poison. "Do you mind if I write in Menal?" I asked. "I have never done any handwriting in Standard." I rarely did any at all, but at least I had practiced calligraphy in school like all Menal children.

"I don't care," he said. He started to pace back and forth in front of me. Then he began to talk. This is the story I wrote:

"My name is Jeff Hope. I was born on the planet Johnson. My mother left after giving birth to my little sister, and my father died when we were still young. And my sister... My dear sister, Lucy, fell into bad company.

She met a man called Enoch Drebber and his right hand, Johanna Stangerson. They were successful business people on the surface, but their fortune was built on drug money. Drebber was older than my sister. He dressed well and talked smoothly. He told my Lucy, bless her soul, that she was the prettiest girl he knew and that he would make her rich. He promised her wealth, and he promised her happiness. All she had to do was work for him as a distributor. She should have declined, but Lucy was in love with Drebber. She would do anything to be near him. So she accepted his proposal and became an associate. A drug dealer. She moved in fancy circles where I, her lowly brother, could not go. She provided high society with drugs and hoped that one day she would be more than someone who just worked for Enoch Drebber. That if she did well, she would win his affection.

But as time went on, she began to soothe her heart with the very drugs she sold. And Drebber, that despicable man, did nothing. He let her sink into addiction and even encouraged her to sample the wares. He led her on. Told her he would marry her when she had done enough to help him secure his fortune. But he never intended to do that. How could he let her abase herself like that if he really loved her? How could he let her slide into abuse if he respected her?

One day, she came to me with happiness sparkling in her eyes and a ring sparkling on her finger. Mr Enoch Drebber had given her the ring with the promise to marry her. She told me he would make the announcement at a party attended by his wealthy friends.

She died alone in a restroom during that party. From an overdose of the drug that immoral hound fed her. Perhaps he killed her deliberately. Perhaps he sent that weak-willed Stangerson to do it. And perhaps it really was an accident, but regardless, Enoch Drebber murdered my sister!"

Chapter XIV
THE AVENGING HUMAN

The murderer, Jeff Hope as he called himself, fell silent. When I looked up from my hastily scribbled notes, his demeanor had changed. His mouth was no longer a hateful line but set in grief, and his eyes were red and wet with the memory.

It suddenly dawned on me that the image of Lucy Hope my mind had formed while I listened to the story was not pure fabrication. I had seen her once before. Only yesterday, as much as it felt like an eternity ago, Jeff Hope's accomplice showed me a still of her when she came to collect the ring. I understood the strange cropping of the picture now. The person next to that happy, smiling young woman must have been Enoch Drebber. Perhaps it had been taken at that very party. Perhaps the Lucy in the still fully believed that Drebber was going to marry her. And perhaps it was taken mere moments before her death.

"I am sorry," I said, meaning it, because the death of Lucy Hope truly was tragic. "What happened after that? You decided to kill Drebber and Stangerson?"

"I took the damned ring off her cold, dead hand," Jeff Hope said. There was a faraway look on his face as if he was not hearing me. "I took it, and I vowed to keep it with me and avenge her. To make those responsible for taking her life tremble with fear. To make them gamble with their lives like they had gambled with hers.

But they left Johnson shortly after to pursue business elsewhere. And I had no choice but to follow. Like the ghost of Lucy Hope, I stalked them. Only one step behind as they moved across the galaxy. I was always in the shadows, taking on jobs where I could to pay for my pursuit, always at their heels and planning my revenge. It was the only thing that mattered. The only thing that drove me.

And then they came to Ganmak."

Jeff Hope did not say another word. I finished my translation and looked up once more. "If you want me to have the full picture, you have to tell me what happened here too," I said as gently as I could.

He bobbed his head in the human affirmative. "I took on odd jobs on my travels to be able to afford following those two. I serviced windows on a zetoi planet once. A dangerous job for a human there. But if I were ever afraid of heights, that cured me."

"I can imagine," I said. Zetois can fly, of course, so their architecture is of the tall variety, and they would not have the safety gear for people working off the ground that their fellow species such as humans and wendek would require. I recalled the drone with the pulley system that Hope so easily used to get into Johanna Stangerson's room in the self-service hotel. That made sense now.

"Between that and Ganmak, I was on another planet where I worked as a cleaner in a laboratory. It was there that I hatched the idea for how exactly my revenge was going to come to fruition. Drebber and Stangerson gambled with people's lives. They gambled with Lucy's life. I was going to give them a taste of their own medicine. So I made a poison."

"You made those capsules yourself?" I asked, perhaps unwisely. "That is impressive."

"So you know about the capsules. I see," Jeff Hope acknowledged. "Well, I found out how to concoct a potent poison. It isn't that hard."

"No, it's not," I agreed. "But not everybody can follow a formula, and turning the compound into regular-looking capsules takes skill and the right tools."

He studied me for a moment that seemed to drag on, those cold, blue eyes boring into mine. "I am beginning to wonder... What do you do if you are not in the peace corps, Kellieth ReinAraneinth?"

I was startled to hear him speak my name. Of course he had guessed I wasn't really called Kelly Reinhardt, but how had he come by my actual identity? "How— How do you know my name?" I asked.

"It took me a while to figure out where I had seen you before with that disguise of yours. Most people would not see beyond species and would probably not make the connection, but as I told you, I never forget a face. And you claim not to be in the peace corps."

"I'm not," I said hurriedly. Where had he seen me before this odious trip out of Nantheam? "I'm just a chemist. A retired chemist."

"Kellieth the chemist." Hope said. "Well, if you lose, I will be sorry."

"You don't have to kill me," I said. "It doesn't have to end like that. Even the human justice system must have some lenience when it comes to this sort of case. You can get a fair trial—"

"Don't you understand?" he cut me off. "I have nothing more to live for."

"If that is true, then why are we here?" I asked. "Excuse my indelicacy, but why have you not killed yourself, then? You have the means. You could have left your story in a number of other ways if you wanted the world to know. Imagine I die and you live. All that has come out of our time here is one more death on your conscience. The death of a person who is not even involved. A person who had no idea Drebber or Stangerson or you even existed a few days ago!"

For a moment, I thought he might see reason. That he might realize I was right and stop all this. Then his face hardened again. "No. This is the way it must be. If I live and you die, then providence has willed it. Then I am supposed to live. If you live, I will have died for my sins."

I know very little about human religions. I know they are the historical and cultural backbone of many communities, and I expect they function in much the same way that our belief systems and myths do. And like ours, I doubt the meaning of them is to justify horrible deeds. But a debate on religion was not going to resolve the situation. As tragic a character as Jeff Hope might be, he had made a choice to personally seek revenge. He had followed his targets for years and eventually killed them. Now I had become an obstacle for him, and he had worked out a way to rationalize why he had to play this game of his with me.

"Your story is not over yet," I said. "Before we do anything else, you need to tell me what happened after you arrived on Ganmak."

Jeff Hope's head tilted up and down again, and he continued:

"I found a job as a rent ride driver. It served to pay my expenses while I waited for the right moment to strike, and it also gave me a way to follow Drebber and Stangerson without raising any suspicion. I waited for them to need a ride and when finally Drebber did, I was there. It was a rainy night, and the man was so drunk he fell asleep in my groundwheeler. As I drove, Lucy sat next to me. She was smiling. Encouraging me.

I took Drebber to an empty house that I had acquired a keycard for earlier when one of the workers forgot it in my groundwheeler. I lit a lamp and told the bastard to look at me. He recognized me. Oh, the fear on his face when he realized who I was! He accused me of wanting to murder him in cold blood, but as I have told you, I only wanted to play a game. He had as much of a chance to leave alive as I did.

But after I had put a poison capsule in one cup of black brew and a harmless one in another, it was he who took the one containing the fatal poison. I watched him writhe about in pain. I watched him die.

When it was over, I dipped my gloved fingers in Drebber's cup of black brew and wrote on the wall. I wanted to leave a message there so someone knew he only got what he deserved. But writing it in English would be giving away too much, and then I was reminded of that draever story of the soldier returning from a war to avenge his whole family. I wrote my message and left." Jeff Hope broke off and looked up at me. "I didn't bother to take Drebber's cup, but I brought my own with me because it was bound to have my DNA on it. I disposed of it elsewhere, in case you were wondering," he said.

I hadn't been, but maybe it would be of interest to Raithan.

He took a deep breath. Closed his blue eyes as if he were gathering strength to tell me the next bit of the story. As I was certainly not in a hurry, I let him take his time.

"Lucy was gone at this point," he finally continued. "I felt for her ring in my pocket where I always keep it and to my horror, it was not there. I stopped my groundwheeler and hurried back on foot. I knew I had it in the house because I showed it to Drebber before he died. I have been carrying it with me for so long, and I have always felt she was still with me, watching over me, but I could not feel her anymore.

I was beside myself with fresh grief until I saw your ad on The Sparkle. I didn't dare go for it myself, so I paid a fellow human rent driver for the trouble. Told her to dress up and make sure no one followed her. I gave her some of my homemade anti-wendek perfume too. It worked splendidly, wouldn't you say?"

So that was where he had seen my face. Of course. If Raithan had been there in that moment, I would have yelled at him. "It did," I agreed, trying to sound soothing, and ignoring my urge to ask him some pointy questions about the so-called anti-wendek perfume. "I am glad I could help. I was never your enemy—"

Jeff Hope made an abortive gesture at me. "Lucy came back, you know," he continued. "When I had the ring back in my possession, my dear baby sister showed herself to me again."

I opened my mouth and then hastily thought the better of it. I am a person of science, but there is much science does not know even in our day and age, and there is much I do not know about humans. I will not dispute with finality that a human spirit can linger after the body's death. What I do know, however, is that the ring Jeff Hope got was a counterfeit, and so even if I accepted that a spirit could be tied to an object, it was clear to me that this iteration of Lucy Hope was nothing but a revenge-driven human's delusions.

"But my work was not done yet. Drebber was dead, but Stangerson still lived. I thought to myself, where would a lone human go on a wendek world? And where would she go to hide because she surely had seen the news that Drebber was dead and was fearing for her own life. I knew I had to find her fast because she might well flee Ganmak again at the first opportunity. I narrowed down her options. She would not go back to the human-owned host house. And she would know that a staffed wendek establishment would be able to smell her unease. Maybe her guilt and her whole history. Who knows what you people can figure out about a person with your uncanny noses?

I found her in a self-service hotel. I disguised myself as a window cleaner, entered through the window of her room and surprised her in bed. I was going to make Johanna Stangerson the same offer that I had made Enoch Drebber. To play the game with me. I doubted that providence would allow her guilty hand to pick the harmless capsule.

But Stangerson was prepared. She jumped at me with a knife, ready to slit my throat. I acted in self-defense when I plunged that very same knife into her heart. I brought it with me and discarded it far away. I dropped the glass with the two capsules in the struggle, but that didn't matter. I had more. And I had Lucy with me because I had her ring.

I returned to my job as a rent driver. A few more weeks of honest work and I would be able to afford to return to Johnson. But then I was summoned to pick you up. Only I did not know it was you until you stepped into my groundwheeler. And you left me no choice."

I stopped writing. "No. I think you had a choice, and I think you still do. Would Lucy want you to kill me?"

He became still then, looking at something behind me, and I did not turn because I knew I would only see trees and water where he saw his sister.

"Lucy understands. And now, Kellieth ReinAraneinth, the time has come."

"Hold on. I need to finish writing the last part," I said, which was a lie. I scribbled as quickly as I could to add some notes for Raithan or whoever found my body if I did not get out of the situation alive. But I had no intention of going along with this game of Hope's peacefully. After all, I had nothing to lose at this point.

CHAPTER XV
A FLIGHT FOR LIFE

Jeff Hope advanced on me and I sprang up, throwing the pen and the papers at him with such a force that they collided with his face in a flurry of white sheets. I turned and I ran.

It will not, I expect, come as a shock to anyone that I was not in great shape at this point in my life, and the logic of attempting to escape was hardly void proof. I knew from the start that I would not be able to backtrack our steps and reach the rent ride before he caught up to me, and continuing further into the Verdant was even more hopeless. I might be able to find a path or a road, but the chances that I would reach help in time were staggeringly low. So my plan, if you can call it a plan, was to use what little advantages I inherently possessed.

Humans are descended from omnivores and predators, but given their bulk and relative stubbiness, I intended to gamble on wendek, even this particular wendek, being superior at scaling and climbing. If I could find a tall tree with branches that could hold my modest weight, I should be able to climb it, and Jeff Hope would be stuck on the ground. That would buy me some time, at least.

But of course my adversary reached me before I even left the clearing at the lake. He tackled me with little effort, and I hit the ground with a thud and a cry of pain and frustration. I rolled over and kicked at every vulnerable spot on his body that I could think of. My one advantage now was the fact that he did not want to murder me or hurt me badly. He wanted to play his game with me. I threw a punch in his face when he bent down to pick me up. Yet, the only reward I got for my efforts consisted of sore knuckles and a coughing fit that left me gasping and all too defenseless.

"That's quite enough!" I heard a voice shout. It was authoritative, and its owner's Standard had a familiar Menal accent. Raithan was here. Raithan was finally here!

I was pulled back to my feet by the scruff of my neck, and Hope held me with one powerful arm around my heaving chest. He slammed his hand across my mouth, and I felt something hard press against my lips. Two capsules.

"Don't make a move or I will kill them!" Hope barked.

Through my struggle to breathe, made worse by the human's fleshy hand against my mouth and nostrils, I saw Raithan stand some ten paces away from us. He was aiming his gun at Hope and everything about him, from his carefully arranged hair to his sleek shoes looked incredibly incongruous in this landscape. I wondered, irrelevantly, if the man had ever gone camping even once in his entire life.

"Drop your weapon!" Hope continued. "I have two capsules in my hand, and one of them will—"

"Yes, yes," Raithan said impatiently. "I'm not stupid, Mr Jeff Hope."

Two thoughts came to my frantic mind. First of all, I wanted to tell Raithan to please not further aggravate the person who was very much capable of killing me, but with Hope's sweaty hand against my mouth and the danger of ingesting the capsules, I couldn't say a word. Secondly, how did he know the human's name when I had only just learned it?

"No, you really are not stupid, are you?" Hope replied. "You're the one pulling the strings on this puppet, aren't you?" Then he actually shook me as if I were nothing but an inanimate object.

"Kellieth is far more than a puppet," Raithan said, which I appreciated despite everything. "But you are right about one thing. My name is Raithan WeinZalneinth, and it is me you want. Not Kellieth."

"Tell me," the murderer replied, "who are you exactly? How do you know my name? I have never met you before."

"As for your name… Well, I came across your vehicle on the way here. I merely read the identifier inside it," Raithan said. "But I assure you this is nothing personal. I am only doing my job."

"So you are in the peace corps, then." Jeff Hope's hand tightened on my face and one of the capsules tried to slip in between my tightly shut lips.

"I'm with the Federal Wendek Security Agency," Raithan corrected him. "I sent Kellieth to lure you to a location of my choosing. So, you see, it really is me you want. I am the one determined to put an end to your criminal activities, not them."

Hope's hand squeezed even tighter. "If you say so. Drop your weapon, or your friend dies."

I wondered if pretending to faint would provide Raithan with a useful distraction, but even as it crossed my mind, I was aware that very soon, I might not have to pretend anything. Hope's hand was tight against my mouth, and his fingers almost blocked my nose too. Without my health issues, breathing like this would be difficult, and for me, the shallow breaths I snatched were far from sufficient. The greenery around us was growing dangerously unsaturated and out of focus. Raithan was speaking, but my head was buzzing too loudly for me to make out what he was saying.

And then I was on my knees, coughing and breathing hard, but breathing. Begging my body not to hyperventilate, not to have an asthma attack because this was not the time. I looked up to see Raithan standing with his empty hands out. His gun was on the ground.

"Are you all right, Kellieth?" he asked.

"Yes," I croaked. "I'm... fine."

"If I lose, do I have your word that you will let Kellieth go?" Raithan asked.

Oh no. I realized he must have agreed to play the game instead of me. "Raithan—" I began.

"Not now." Raithan did not look at me. His face was set, and he did not appear to be nervous, but there was something off about him, I now saw. His breathing was as irregular and quick as mine, and his face was glistening with sweat. Perhaps he had been running hard to catch up with us. But he was also oddly pale, so that did not add up. "Well, Hope? Do we have a deal?" he asked.

"I need to make sure I'm not followed."

"That is reasonable," Raithan said. "I have an idea. I'm going to take something from my pocket. It is not another weapon." He reached slowly into his jacket and retrieved a set of handcuffs. "If I lose, you can cuff Kellieth to me. They aren't nearly strong enough to drag my corpse along."

"Raithan!" I cried because I could not think of anything worse than being handcuffed to Raithan's dead body, except, of course, his being dead in the first place. "Don't do this!"

"It's all right, my dear Kellieth," Raithan said, giving me one quick smile. "I am very good at this sort of game. Now, be quiet and let me concentrate."

On what? It was a game of chance. Even someone as brilliant as Raithan needed a way to figure out which capsule was the harmless one. If Hope himself knew, Raithan probably would be able to read the human's scents well enough to discern the identity of the pills, but Hope had palmed both of them, and there was simply no way he could know. I had examined the siblings of those capsules, and I knew that only a chemical analysis or ingestion would reveal which was which. Did Raithan have a different plan? He might pretend to take one and keep it in his mouth instead of swallowing, but this was a quickly dissolving substance. I should have told him that. Why hadn't I told him that?

Hope held out his hand, and Raithan stepped closer. He studied the hand, then looked at Hope thoughtfully.

"Pick one, wendek," Hope said.

"I will," Raithan said. His voice did not betray any emotions at all. How could he be so calm?

"Well?" Hope urged him.

Raithan reached out and let his hand hover above Hope's for a moment. It trembled. Then he picked up one capsule and held it up for his opponent to see.

"Raithan," I tried once more. "Please don't!" Although in retrospect, I appreciate that the only other option was me taking the pill, which I really did not want to, either.

"Ready?" Raithan asked Hope.

"Let us see if I am meant to be absolved or if I am to meet my maker," Hope said.

Simultaneously and agonizingly slowly, they took a capsule each. As I watched, they both dry-swallowed. The ceremonious nature of the whole thing would have been funny if not for the fact that there was a 50 percent chance that my neighbor and friend had just killed himself.

I got to my feet. The moment stretched out far beyond its chronological boundaries. Whatever was going to happen now would happen. I could try to make Raithan throw up, but these capsules were designed to act quickly. If he had swallowed the poison, all I could hope for was being fast enough to catch him in my arms when he collapsed.

"Right shoe," Raithan said to me. "Be quick."

Chapter XVI
CHEMICAL CONCOCTIONS

I was trying to work out the meaning of Raithan's words when Jeff Hope gave an exclamation of pain or surprise or both. "You win," he groaned. "And I—" His words turned into a ghastly gurgling.

I never imagined I could feel profound relief at another person's demise. Nevertheless, when I saw that sad and wretched human Jeff Hope stumble and fall to his knees in what was clearly the prelude to his death, it was as if I could suddenly breathe again. Which is a sensation with which I am intimately familiar.

Raithan bent down and pulled up his pant leg, and the meaning of his words became clear to me. He had a disposable inhaler strapped to his ankle.

"Antidote?" I asked.

"Yes," Raithan said. "He is not getting out of this so easily. Can you..?" His hands were trembling worse than when he took the capsule from Hope. I had never seen his hands unsteady before. He must be more agitated than he let on.

I took the inhaler. It felt oddly appropriate that I should be the one to administer the antidote in this form. Unlike my own device, this one was flimsy and cheaply printed. It was the kind you might keep in your home for an emergency if you knew you had an allergy to something but didn't expect to have to use it. However, the principle was exactly the same. Breathe in the medication, and it would work almost immediately. Probably it was made for wendek, but humans are physically so close to us that I had no doubt they could inhale the contents of the device too.

Hope was making horrible noises and thrashed on the ground in his would-be death throes. Raithan held him still while I placed the inhaler and forced the him to breathe in the contents. I was never on this side of the procedure before, but I had been on the receiving end enough times to know how it went.

"Help should be here soon," Raithan said, oddly breathlessly. "Excuse me."

"Where are you going?" I asked.

But Raithan only stood and went a few paces away, reaching out to steady himself on the tree I meant to climb earlier. Something definitely was wrong with him. Could both capsules have contained poison? No, Raithan would have reacted as violently as Hope if that were the case.

"Raithan?" I called after him.

He did not reply. Instead he bent over and vomited. On the ground beside me, Hope was doing the same without any of my neighbor's self-control. I tried to keep him from injuring himself with his convulsive movements the best I could. The stench was utterly repulsive.

Raithan returned, wiping at his mouth with a scented tissue.

"Sit down," I told him.

"I'm fine," he said.

"I am familiar with that kind of fine!" I snapped because I was. It was the kind where you told yourself you were fine because you were not dying or seriously injured and did not want to admit you needed help or rest out of fear of appearing weak. "Sit down!"

Raithan grinned at me, but the usual sharp edges of that grin were somewhat weakened by his general appearance. "You are giving me orders," he observed, but he did sit down next to me.

"Please," croaked Jeff Hope. "Please, let me go. Let me die."

"No," Raithan said. "You are going to face justice for killing Enoch Drebber and Johanna Stangerson."

"He was avenging his sister," I said, as irrelevantly righteous as that was.

Raithan tilted his head back and exhaled. "That is not relevant at the moment. It is not up to me to look at mitigating circumstances. That is a job for the judicature."

Hope was moaning, but he was thrashing about less now, and I was not sure if it were a good or a bad sign.

"You took the antidote too, didn't you?" I asked Raithan. With the two of them exhibiting similar symptoms, I could not help drawing that conclusion.

"Yes," Raithan said. "A smaller dose, but I wanted to be prepared since I anticipated we were going to play his game."

"Of course you did."

"Here." Raithan reached into his jacket and produced my inhaler.

"Thank you," I said. My breathing was fine right now, so I merely stuffed into my own pocket.

"It appears you had a nosebleed. Are you all right?"

I wiped at my upper lip and, indeed, facepaint and dried blood came off. "Yes. To both," I said because I couldn't start telling him about the ride to the Verdant here and now. "I'm not injured or anything."

"That's good. I must say, dear Kellieth, that I was touched to smell how fervently you didn't want me to die," Raithan continued, and although his smile was only an approximation of his usual charm, it was still enough to make me wish I could hide my scents from him.

"You said help is on the way?" I changed the subject.

"I did. And— ah, yes, here they are."

Before I could ask any more questions, the whining of a sphereflier's rotating wings made me look up. The round transport was quickly approaching us from the direction of Nantheam, disturbing the leaves of the canopies around us as it slowed, probably searching for a suitable place to land. From its bright colors and markings, it appeared to be an emergency flier.

"Can you retrieve the papers before any of them fly off?" Raithan asked.

"Right," I said and climbed to my feet. Despite everything, I felt steady enough as I began to pick up the testimony I had thrown in Hope's face. One of the sheets almost did fly off as the sphereflier's altitude decreased and its wings stirred up a spontaneous wind. I scrambled after the paper and snatched it up before it went into the lake.

The flier circled once, then apparently gave up and went into hovering mode instead. A hatch opened, and three figures began to descend using ropes and an automatic pulley system. Two of them wore medical service uniforms, and the third sported a familiar red braid that whipped around her.

"Status, please," shouted one of the medics to me over the noise of the sphereflier as soon as he touched the ground. The other went straight to Jeff Hope with Lystrath.

"The human was poisoned," I said and continued to list the hathnitrate, its density and my estimate of the amount in the capsule.

"When?" the medic asked.

"Around 15 minutes ago." My best estimate without a patch. I looked at Raithan for confirmation.

"Just over 14 minutes," he specified.

"I administered a general antidote immediately after," I continued, holding out the disposable inhaler to the medic. "He is going to need intravenous fluids and— and you know that because that's your job," I added, deflating a little.

"Thank you," the medic said and took what I handed him. He looked down at Raithan. "And you?"

"I'm perfectly all right," Raithan said, almost a little peevishly that other people kept doubting this. He did not look particularly all right.

"He took a preemptive and smaller dose of the same antidote but has ingested no poison," I clarified.

"And you... What happened to you?" the medic asked me.

"Nothing," I said. Which was not at all accurate. I had been abducted, drugged, dragged around, thrown on the ground, held hostage, threatened, scared witless ... And I had had a nosebleed and was also still mostly beige, and that was probably what he was referring to. "I was disguised as a human," I explained. "But I am not injured. Please do concentrate on the others."

The medic accepted this, probably because I was the only one standing up, and went to quickly talk to the other medic before he bent down to examine Raithan.

Lystrath turned to us. "What the thak happened?" she asked me. "How did you end up here?"

"It's a very long story," I said.

"That is the person who murdered Enoch Drebber and Johanna Stangerson," Raithan said, making a vague gesture to indicate Hope. The paramedic was handing him a bottle. "And Kellieth took a written confession from him."

"That's nice," Lystrath said dismissively before looking at me again. "But why are you even here? Why are you dressed up as a human?"

"I... The murderer was a rent ride driver. I pretended to be a fellow human customer, so Raithan could apprehend him..." I trailed off. It sounded completely ridiculous now. It had seemed to make perfect sense at the time, but how had that been the most prudent method? Couldn't Raithan have investigated the rent ride company and have them identify Hope for him? Or let his Irregulars track Hope's groundwheeler? Something like that.

Lystrath's nostrils flared and she stared at Raithan. "You used your friend as bait? Raithan WeinZalneinth, are you completely out of your mind?"

"I assure you that everything was under control. I had my Irregulars track the rent ride through public surveillance systems as long as it was in Nantheam, and I also placed a tracker on Kellieth in case they went off script, which they did. I never meant for them to be in any danger," Raithan said.

That was news to me. I had hoped he might be able to use his Irregulars to locate my patch, but a tracker on me? I thought back to his adjusting the human shirt I was wearing. Was that when he planted it? I felt inside the front pocket and indeed, there was a tiny device sticking to the fabric.

I almost shouted at Raithan, then, telling him that very clearly, I had been in danger. And not only that, I had also been thakking scared. But somehow I couldn't. Not now. The medic was checking his pulse and blood pressure, and Raithan was looking miserable clutching the water bottle he had been given. And Lystrath was already throwing him a stink bomb over this whole thing.

"Did Greithon tell you Kellieth is my friend?" Raithan asked, an obvious attempt to throw her off course.

"Yes. Don't think I'm not annoyed with you for letting me believe they are your assistant."

"They happen to be a Doyen of chemistry, and they have assisted me—" Raithan began.

"All right, so you had the human murderer drive Kellieth to this place, and then what?" Lystrath asked acerbically over whatever he would have said next. I was uncertain whether her anger stemmed from concern for me, or if this was the continuation of an older argument about Raithan's methods.

Raithan explained what had happened from his point of view. Apparently, he waited in the original location until he saw both my patch and the tracker he had planted on me go in the wrong direction. Footage from public surveillance, via his Irregulars, had shown the rent ride heading for the outskirts of Nantheam.

Then he had followed as quickly as possible, but traffic and distance meant he had ended up far behind Hope and me. In fact, the traffic had been so slow that he managed to locate my patch and pick it up from the side of the road on the way. And then he had not gotten very far into the Verdant before his groundwheeler got thoroughly stuck in the soft, wet ground. It was a city vehicle that was not meant for off-roading, so Raithan had to continue on foot. He came across the rent ride on the way and picked up my inhaler.

When he arrived in the clearing and saw Hope talking and me writing, he waited to see what would happen because I did not appear to be in any immediate danger, as he put it. Once we were done, he knew he would not be able to save me without taking my place, so he took a preemptive dose of the antidote.

"That is the most ridiculous plan I have ever heard," Lystrath said when Raithan stopped talking. "Aren't you supposed to be smarter than the rest of us?"

Raithan had the decency to look slightly abashed. "I get carried away," he said.

"If you knew the murderer was a human rent ride driver, you must have been able to find him without all those... shenanigans," she continued.

"It was a bit more complicated than that," Raithan said. "Jeff Hope killed two people, and he knew someone might be on his scent. He is smart and cunning. He would have bolted the moment the company recalled him or law enforcement showed up at his door."

Lystrath shook her head in disbelief. "Still. You are a menace, Raithan, and you need someone to keep your nose on the ground," she said.

Raithan looked up sharply, and I saw something pass between them. A keener sense of smell than mine would probably have caught some of the meaning.

"Investigator," the medic said to Lystrath. "We need to get the human to a hospital."

"Yes," she agreed. "Go. My colleague will be here shortly. Can you take those two with you?" she added.

"I don't need medical attention," I said because one thing I have gained from my health problems is being very good at correctly assessing my own condition. I knew I was running on the natural chemicals a wendek body produces under stress, and I would feel exhausted soon. But I was not seriously injured. "I need a shower and rest, that's all."

"I concur," Raithan said. "I've had worse."

Lystrath and the medic grudgingly accepted this. I wanted to ask Raithan what he thought of as worse. I didn't.

We watched in silence as the medics fastened Hope to a collapsible stretcher. His head lolled to the side, and despite his condition, the human's eyes fixed on me. "I did what I had to," he all but whispered. "For Lucy. It was all for Lucy. Please... Please tell them about her."

I pressed my lips together. What Jeff Hope did was undeniably despicable. But a small part of me felt sorry for him all the same. Pitied him that he had gone to such lengths and destroyed lives for no other reason than his own overwhelming grief. "I wrote down everything you told me," I said. That was all the relief I would or could give him.

Then the medics finished their preparations, and they ascended to the sphereflier with their patient. The hatch barely closed before it took off. In its absence, we heard a groundwheeler approaching.

Greithon's blustering blue vehicle's large wheels and general sturdiness looked out of place in the nature reservation, but it was well-suited for the soft, uneven ground. He sprang out of it and jogged up to us. "What the thak happened?" he asked. "Why are you beige?" The last bit for me, obviously.

Raithan climbed to his feet and looked like he might throw up again, but he kept down the water the medic had forced him to drink. "So good of you to finally join us," he said to Greithon, sounding like Greithon was late for an appointment. "I already told Lystrath my part of the tale, and I will personally debrief Kellieth once we get back and they have the chance to recover from this ordeal."

Lystrath caught my eye. We were thinking the same thing, I was sure. "Yes, once I recover," I repeated.

"I will guide you to the murderer's rent ride," Raithan continued to Greithon, "and as my own groundwheeler needs some assistance getting out of the Verdant, I would be much obliged if you would be so kind as to take the two of us home."

"Do you live together?" Greithon asked.

"We are neighbors," I replied, inwardly cringing at how much that sounded like a popular trope.

Chapter XVII
THE CONCLUSION

By the time we reached our building, the excitement of the day's events had subsided, and I was incredibly weary. I murmured my thanks to Greithon and Lystrath and tried in vain to keep from visibly trembling. Raithan, on the contrary, was looking better, and it was he who supported me on our way up the stairs where we met for the first time.

"Kellieth," he said as I unlocked the door to my apartment with my temporary key card. I had meant to ask Hussa when my retina scan was likely to go through, but my mind had been entirely occupied with Raithan's case for several days.

Despite my fatigue, I turned to look at him because there was something unfamiliar in his voice. "Yes? Are you all right?"

"I am. But— No," Raithan cut himself off. "It can wait. Here is your patch."

I took it without a word. It looked perfectly fine despite being torn off my wrist and thrown out of a groundwheeler. The advantage of prioritizing practicality over fashion, I suppose.

"What do you need right now?" What did I need him to do for me, he meant.

"I need to be alone," I told him bluntly because I really did. I needed not to look at Raithan WeinZalneinth for a moment longer. I needed to wash and drink a comforting mug of black brew, and I needed to sleep.

"Understood," he said, and I think he actually did. "When you are ready, you know where to find me."

I woke up the next morning feeling less exhausted and more sore all over. I had no injuries to speak of, only a few bruises on my upper arm and knees, but I was not used to physical exertion these days. I was, especially, not used to having to fight other people.

I was half surprised that Raithan wasn't knocking on my door or sending me dispatches asking me how I felt or inviting me for breakfast. But then, I had told him to leave me alone. He apparently chose today to respect my boundaries. So I made breakfast for myself and checked the news while I ate.

A human called Jeff Hope had been arrested for the murders of his fellow humans Enoch Drebber and Johanna Stangerson, the news told me. First Class Investigator Lystrath NefNenenth and Second Class Investigator Greithon OenKelneinth of the Nantheam peace corps had tracked him down and chased him to the Verdant where they had overpowered him as he was about to kill himself with the very same poison he had used on his victims. On him, he had a written statement detailing the circumstances and motivations for his crimes. He had been taken into custody and would be tried by the judicature and most likely deported to his homeworld as soon as he was well enough.

"Oh, come on!" I exclaimed. Not a word about Raithan. Not a word about me. Not even a brief mention of a FWSA agent challenging Hope or a chemist disguised as a human actually penning the confession. I knew Raithan accepted it, even preferred to reside in the shadows, but he could remain anonymous and still be given some credit. It smelled utterly wrong that the peace corps got to reap the renown for everything. I couldn't help wondering how often that happened. How often I watched the news and only got half of the truth, not because of some political agenda, but simply because a federal agent had slipped away and allowed the peace corps to bask in the glory.

I swiped the display out of existence with more force than necessary and washed down the news with a mouthful of black brew. It wasn't that I necessarily wanted to be interviewed and praised for my involvement. After all, what was I but a pawn that Raithan had deployed and played? Hope had called me his puppet, and despite Raithan's protestations, wasn't that exactly what I was?

I stood up with a wince, walked past the pile of human-style clothes I had deposited over the back of a chair the previous day, and went to look out of my window. It was another day of showers in Nantheam. As I watched, a couple ran across the street, laughing and splashing water from the puddles as they reached the other side. Someone hurried past, shielding a package from the local bakery from the rain with their jacket.

It was an ordinary day. If any of those people had seen the news about Jeff Hope, it was just another crime, irrelevant to their personal lives. Three humans had come to Ganmak, and one had killed the two others. He had been caught, and it had absolutely nothing to do with any of them. Why should they care?

But it had everything to do with me. And I was going to have to self-diagnose and find out how best to deal with it. I closed my eyes and listened to the rain. I was expecting trauma, but I couldn't find any. Yes, I had been scared for my life, for Raithan's life, and maybe I would resent rent rides a little bit from now on. Yesterday was very emotional and taxing. But I knew what shape trauma took in my mind, and it was not there. I was not in shock, not repressing my emotions or longing to unburden myself.

Next, I turned my attention to Raithan or, more accurately, my emotions regarding him. And they were, perhaps unsurprisingly, a tangle. It was not that I was unsure how I felt. I only felt a lot of different and somewhat conflicting things. The utter relief when Raithan showed up to save me from Jeff Hope. The anger at him because I felt used. The terror when I understood he meant to play the game instead of me. And then relief and anger once more when it turned out that he had the antidote...

What surprised me was my own reaction to it all. When we parted the previous day, I expected never wanting to have anything to do with Raithan WeinZalneinth again. From his point of view, he had probably acted perfectly logically, but as interesting and intelligent as the man was, he was also dangerous. Not only to criminals but also, as I had experienced first-hand, to those who got close to him. Those who got embroiled in his schemes to exact justice. And yet, I had to talk to him. I had to at least attempt to conclude matters between us.

I decided to get it over with. Looking in the mirror as I arranged my hair, I noticed that my reflection looked... good. I am aware that I am normally considered a fairly attractive specimen of our species despite my faults, but I had become so used to seeing my own haggard and exhausted expression. This morning I had regained some of the vitality that my experiences on Almaimak had stripped from me. It was both a wonderful and an aggravating feeling because I very well knew why.

I finished my preparations and went to our common room. Raithan was not there waiting for me, which gave me some satisfaction. Judging by the muffled sound coming from his apartment, he was currently playing his mewienn. I crossed the space and stopped by his door. It was unlocked. I steeled myself, straightened up and opened it.

The volume of the music increased as I entered. I quietly followed the sound into his living room where the battered instrument case lay open on the table. Despite having heard him play before, being in the room with him was a quite different experience.

The mewienn was the old sort, made from real wood. It was unfolded and rested on the floor in the middle of the room. Raithan stood with his eyes closed, gently swaying as he produced the most beautiful notes with the antiquated instrument. He looked peaceful.

I did not recognize the melody, but the sound of those resonant strings brought me back to my childhood lessons in traditional Menal dance once more. Why could I not help longing to dance to his tune? Yes, I know. The incredibly trite metaphor was not lost on me, either.

Raithan had probably smelled my presence, but he continued playing until the music reached a natural conclusion. Then he opened his eyes. Yesterday's pallor was gone from his face, and he looked as healthy as ever.

"That was beautiful," I said, which was not at all the words I had come to say.

Raithan acknowledged this with a small bow and folded the mewienn with the ease of an expert.

"I hope I didn't interrupt you," I continued, which was also not even remotely what I meant to say.

"No, I was expecting you," he said.

And I snapped right back to being irritated with him. "Of course you were."

"How do you feel? Do you want to sit?"

"I'm fine." I was not going to let him distract me. "I'm here for my debriefing."

"Of course," he said and carefully put the instrument back in its case.

"And also," I pressed on, "You used me."

"Yes, because you agreed to the plan," Raithan said. He was looking at me levelly now. I wished I could smell what he was feeling.

"You didn't tell me the plan. Or you did, but not all of it. You placed a tracker on me. That would have been very nice to know. And you made me think you would die if you took the wrong capsule. You —"

"Kellieth," Raithan said. "I put a tracker on you to make sure I wouldn't lose you if something happened to your patch or you went somewhere without surveillance for my Irregulars to tap. And at the time, I did not know if you were a good enough actor to keep it from the murderer if you knew. I never meant for you to be in any danger."

"Well, I clearly was!" I nearly shouted.

"Were you, though?"

"You need a statement from me, right?" I said. "Well, here it is!" And I went on to describe how Hope had recognized me from my Sparkle profile despite the disguise, how he had thought I was an undercover peace corps officer, how he had decided to play his deadly game with me. How I had panicked in the rent ride and been vapor drugged as a result.

As Raithan listened to all this, his expression grew darker. By the end of my tale, he looked positively ferocious. "If I had known that when I confronted him, I am afraid Jeff Hope would have met his end in the Verdant," he said, and his tone chilled me to the bone. "I have sworn an oath to take any measures necessary to protect my people, and I am sure putting a kinetic projectile in that human's brain on the spot could have been considered such a measure. I am sorry, Kellieth. I never meant for you to come to any harm."

For all his usual flippancy and sarcasm and easy-going manners, and despite my inability to smell his intent, there was not a shadow of doubt in my mind that Raithan WeinZalneinth meant every word. I had considered him dangerous before, but now I saw that he was far more dangerous than I had assumed. This was not a mask or an act. The fierceness and earnestness always lay beneath his calm surface. He would do anything in his power to save what and whom he cared about.

Raithan looked away. Got his expression under control. "I could claim that if you had trusted me and done exactly what I told you, he would not have felt it necessary to subdue you," he said, "but I realize it was an error on my part to expect you to remain entirely calm."

"I—" I suddenly did feel the need to sit down and did so on the couch I had sat on the first time I visited my neighbor to awkwardly thank him for helping me. Had it really been less than a month? "Do you need any further statements from me, or..?"

"Not at this time," Raithan said, slipping back into his usual tone of voice. "Hope is recovering, and I will testify at the judicature in a few days. I expect he will be shipped back to his home planet without any delay. And then this whole business will be over with."

"Good," I said. There was a lot more I had intended to say, but I couldn't quite formulate it now.

Raithan sat down opposite me, and we were both silent for a length of time. "I read the statement you wrote on Hope's behalf," he said.

"I expected you would."

"My compliments on your handwriting and narrative style," he said.

I huffed. Was he being sarcastic to make up for his previous emotional outburst? I had seen his handwriting, and it was a lot more neat and even than mine. "Look, I never did advanced calligraphy, and besides, I was under a lot of pressure! And I thought I might die," I protested.

"Kellieth," Raithan said softly. "I mean it. Even in that stressful situation, your hand was steady, and it takes skill to turn another person's statement into enjoyable prose. And I recognize you must have been translating into Menal simultaneously. Moreover, your final notes were... touching."

"Oh. I— Thank you," I stammered because honestly, what else could I say? "I've been wondering," I added, "about some of the things Lystrath and Greithon said."

"Oh?" Raithan leaned back on the couch, watching me carefully.

"When we first met them, Greithon welcomed you back, and Lystrath said she didn't know you were on duty again. Also, the guard at your headquarters—"

"Ah, all that." Raithan interrupted me with a dismissive gesture. "I was on leave for a while, but I decided to cut it short when Greithon contacted me about the first murder."

"On leave," I repeated. Lystrath had also asked if he was ready to be back, which meant my enigmatic neighbor was probably not merely enjoying a vacation.

"I would be a hypocrite if I did not compliment you on noticing those details of our exchanges," Raithan continued. He was giving me an awful lot of compliments today, and I was not entirely sure if I should be glad or worried. "And on that note, Kellieth, I have something to ask you."

"Go ahead," I said.

"I need an assistant. Do you want to work for me?"

The apartment was silent but for the insistent rain lashing at the windows. I was staring at Raithan, and I fear I smelled as confused and incredulous as I felt.

Raithan's expression was sincere. "I am not asking you to become an agent. You are not fit for service for a number of reasons. But I need someone to organize things, set up meetings, take calls, write and submit reports, that sort of work."

"A secretary, then?" I surmised.

"Partly that. But over the past few days, I have studied you, and you possess skills that would be valuable to me. Your tenacity, your analytical skills, your expertise as a chemist. Your ability to ask relevant questions and your considerable levelheadedness under pressure. I need someone like, well, you." He smiled. "First class agents get to pick their own assistants wherever and however they choose. You will be screened by the Agency, but seeing as I already VoidSearched you, looked for any criminal records and broke through your patch security, I already know you have the relevant qualifications and pass all the tests."

"I—" I swallowed. He was back to being infuriating again, but...

"You miss your work, but your health won't allow you to return to field studies in foreign environments," he continued, ruthlessly honest. "As my assistant, you will at least get access to any equipment you want and do some meaningful lab work, and you will get to exercise your mental capacities. During quiet periods, you can even pursue your own areas of interest in your field. It would be logical to accept my offer."

"I'm a scientist, but I don't solely operate on logic," I said.

"And that is part of the reason I need you."

He... needed me. This blatant declaration made me feel appreciated and pleasantly warm. But I had to view it from another angle as well. Ignore Raithan's needs for a moment.

I leaned back on the couch and looked at the ceiling as if an answer might be written there. Raithan was entirely right. A job like that was probably the best offer I would ever get. I always wanted to make a difference, and as his assistant, I would be able to do that, albeit in a much different way from what I had imagined. An old, familiar voice in the back of my head suggested that perhaps he was only doing this out of charity. Because he felt sorry for his poor, disabled neighbor and recognized that they needed a purpose. But that was simply not Raithan's style. He was offering me a job because he legitimately believed I would be an asset to him. He actually did need me. And I needed—

"Before you answer, I should tell you what happened to my previous assistant," he interrupted my thoughts.

I righted myself again and stared at him. "Yes?"

"He fell in love with me."

A laugh burst out of me. "I'm sorry," I said. "I was expecting some dramatic and tragic demise. You didn't want to work with him because he fell in love with you? Or he couldn't take the unrequited feelings and quit?"

"No, nothing as banal as that. He stopped arguing with me," Raithan clarified. "He stopped asking me questions and calling me out when I made dubious decisions. I meant what I said to Lystrath. I get carried away. I need to be able to bounce ideas off my assistant and get somewhat intelligent answers. Someone who tells me I'm flawless is useless to me."

"Right," I said, deciding to put it to the test. "I can see how that would be a problem. You get caught up in your own brilliant mind and forget other people's feelings. You are rude and patronizing and ostentatious. I could make a list of your many talents, Raithan, but I could certainly also make one of your flaws."

"See?" Raithan grinned at me. "As my assistant, you have to take orders, but you also have to be critical."

"All right. Yes," I said.

"Yes?" he echoed.

"Yes, First Class Independent Agent Raithan WeinZalneinth, I accept your job offer," I specified.

Raithan's posture relaxed. "Good," he said. And then, "I had expected that you would because according to both my nose and my deductions while we were working on the case, you enjoyed yourself much of the time. My study of you indicated—"

"I'm sorry," I cut in, "your study of *me*?"

"Didn't I tell you so when we started?" Raithan asked, incredibly smugly even for him. "It was a study in black brew."

I groaned, and then I laughed. I was starting to get the feeling that these past few days had somehow been an elaborate job interview that I was blissfully unaware of at the time. "Is it too early for me to demand a substantial raise for putting up with you?" It occurred to me that I had not even thought to ask him about my salary.

"It is," he replied, "but I can compensate you for your work assisting me so far."

I considered this. "Can you get me more of that delicious black brew you treated me to yesterday?"

"Certainly," Raithan said. "I can get you anything you want."

I couldn't help grinning. "I'll remember you said that."

Acknowledgements

This is the literary equivalent of a movie's end credits where I get to thank all the awesome people who made *A Study in Black Brew* a reality.

Thank you to Spaceboy Books for believing in my stories and letting me be part of the family. My gratitude to Nate Ragolia especially for doing his editorial magic and making my books the best that they can be. And thank you to Miblart who made a cover that makes me think it's okay to judge this book by it.

As always, I am grateful to my wonderfully supportive family and friends who always have my back, and give me a space to rant about all the people living in the future/my mind.

Very special thanks to my team of beta and sensitivity readers, Chris Balz, Christie Wilson, Gabe Clark, Hanna, Larna Holmes, Malene Marley Neergaard Momme, @naomisnovelnest, Philippe Moret, Sam Buchanan, Thomas Nielsen and Tiara Lockhart for providing me with fantastic feedback, asking all the right questions, and loving my wendek duo.

Also thank you to my Patreon and Ko-fi supporters Gabe Clark, Ryan Watt, Skjalm, ZombiEdward, Aden Ng, Jeanett, and more. You rock!

No acknowledgments are complete without my love to my little cat gang, Reid, Dandy and Oscar, who keep me company and purr everything better (and occasionally nap on my keyboard or block my view of the screen, which is all part of their charm).

And — thank you! I hope you've enjoyed this adventure, and that you will join me for the next one.

Finally, this book literally would not exist without the original Sherlock Holmes story, *A Study in Scarlet*, by Sir Arthur Conan Doyle. So my thanks, sent back in time to Victorian London, for creating some of the most iconic and famous literary figures and stories. And particularly for making Holmes and Watson such great matches for Raithan and Kellieth!

Coming back from the interview with Raithan's employers that formally established my position as his assistant, I stopped short when we reached our landing.

"What is all that?" I asked. A pile of boxes was leaning against my door.

"Improvements to your apartment," Raithan said. "I hope everything you need is there. If not, let me know and I will arrange for it to be delivered."

"Did you... buy me furniture?" I asked. That was overstepping a lot of boundaries.

Raithan smiled. "I could not be more indifferent to your taste in furniture," he said, deducing exactly what I was thinking. "Go on, open one." He handed me a folding knife.

I cut the tape on the top box. Opening it and peering inside, my breath caught in surprise. "This is— lab equipment."

"I'm glad. It would be annoying if they had accidentally shipped a syraxh to you," Raithan said.

"No, but," I insisted, "it's lab equipment. For me?"

"I don't see anyone else here who could have a use of it. We don't want to rely on my skills in that department."

"But I thought I would be using the Agency's facilities?"

"And you will if you need something that doesn't fit in those boxes. But I'm an independent agent, you're my assistant, and that means I get to equip you so you can do your job wherever you want or need to."

"Thank you," I said. I don't doubt he could smell how much I appreciated it. "I need to get this inside and have a look. Will you help me?"

"Of course. I'm glad you asked," Raithan said.

About the Author

Marie Howalt grew up near Copenhagen in Denmark and decided to become a writer at the age of 11 when the local library ran out of science fiction and fantasy to read.

After graduating from the university with a master's degree in religion and English studies with a primary focus on speculative literature, Marie wrote as a hobby and worked as a teacher and a translator between English and Danish before veering onto a different path in life due to chronic illness (post concussion syndrome).

Now, Marie writes as much as physically possible. The stories tend to be hopeful and diverse and take place in the far future or other worlds.

When not writing (or bribing imaginary people to tell their stories), Marie is dedicated to being a cat servant, but also enjoys reading (mostly audiobooks) as well as drawing and restoring antique fountain pens. You can find Marie pushing art supplies, stationary and fancy pens part-time in one of Copenhagen's oldest shops.

Marie's debut novel from Spaceboy Books, *We Lost the Sky*, came out in 2019. Since then, there has been a steady flow of a new book each year (plus the odd short story). *A Study in Black Brew* is a retelling of the classic Sherlock Holmes story *A Study in Scarlet*. It is Marie's seventh book, and while it is a standalone, it is also a spinoff from the *Colibri Investigations* series.

If you want to keep up with Marie's life, writing, and cats, @mhowalt on Instagram is the indisputably best place to go. You can also get special perks and previews by newsletter or on Ko-fi via www.mhowalt.dk

About the Publishers

Nate Ragolia is a lifelong lover of science fiction and its power to imagine worlds more hopeful and inclusive than the real one. His first book, *There You Feel Free*, was published by 1888's Black Hill Press in 2015. Spaceboy Books reissued it in 2021. He's also the author of *The Retroactivist* (2017). His most recent book, *One Person Can't Make a Difference* (2022), was featured on Tor.com's Can't Miss Indie Press Speculative Fiction list, and was translated into Italian for Ringworld Sci-Fi in 2023. He founded and edited *BONED*, a literary magazine, and also created two webcomics. Nate is also a husband and a dog dad.

Shaunn Grulkowski has been compared to Warren Ellis and Phillip K. Dick and was once described as what a baby conceived by Kurt Vonnegut and Margaret Atwood would turn out to be. He's at least the fifth best Slavic-Latino-American sci-fi writer in the Baltimore metro area. He's the author *Retcontinuum*, and the editor of *A Stalled Ox* and *The Goldfish* for 1888/Black Hill Press.